Not a Showmance

First Paperback Edition Sep 2023

ISBN: 979-8-9863386-4-4(paperback)

Published by Birdcage Ink
www.Birdcageink.com

Not a Showmance

A Sapphic RomCom

Stephanie Jean

For my little bug – my first book, for my first born.
I love you.

Act One

"Every knot was once a straight rope."
- Mysterious Man, from *Into the Woods*

"Every thing you lose is a step you take."
- Taylor Swift, "You're on Your Own Kid"

Chapter 1

There was a single fluorescent light flickering incessantly in the small office. "I understand, Mr. Middletop. Unfortunately, there is nothing I can do." Valerie massaged her forehead with her right hand as she adjusted the phone with her left.

"Look, I'm not trying to be an asshole," Mr. Middletop continued, even though he had very much been an asshole since calling, "but I have been very patient. I was told that your marketing team would take pictures of yesterday's event. Jorge was here, he should have them."

Valerie looked at the clock; it was still only 10:30 a.m. and she did not go to lunch until noon. "Of course," she said.

"So where are my pictures?" Mr. Middletop fumed, "Jorge was supposed to get them back to me."

"If you refer to our contract, we have a three-to-five business day turnaround for photos," she said, her words dripping like honey. "Since the event was yesterday, we will not have the photos ready at this time. If you do not receive them by the end of the five-business day window, please call me and I will make sure to get them to you. But for now, we just need to be patient."

"Well, you tell Jorge to call me. Or even the person he sent yesterday."

Valerie looked through her window to Jorge's desk. He had been at a concert last night, so she wasn't surprised when he failed to show up today. "I will let him know to call you as soon as he's available; is there anything else I can do for you?"

Valerie Ross worked for a marketing company named SPRUCE, specifically in the social media department. Technically, she had been hired to be a profile builder. A builder's job is to help clients start their social media presence and build their own businesses or empires or what have you. But once she started working, she got shuffled into Reception and Editorial. While Editorial might sound like it's a step up, it really means that Valerie has been doomed to pick up the scraps that everyone else leaves behind - like copying hashtags no one else bothered to, or talking to clients when their profile builder didn't want to. Which is why she had spent twenty minutes on the phone in her office that barely fit her desk and a filing cabinet. She listened as Mr. Middletop went on and on, and she tried to ignore the flickering light above her head that was causing a migraine.

Once Mr. Middletop was appeased, she checked her email, drafted a caption for a client with a fairy-themed bakery business, and replaced the toner in the copy machine. *Why am I always the one to do this? Everyone gets the notification that the toner is low.*

Her office was right next to the kitchen, so every time someone put their leftovers in the microwave, she could smell it. She had to remember to buy a candle or something. The four walls of her storage closet turned office were the only walls in the building that had never been painted. They were grey-toned with spackle strips marking the beams in the walls. Not exactly cozy.

"What do you think about me putting up wallpaper or some paint in my office?" Valerie had once asked a coworker during her first few months at SPRUCE. "That could be nice," she had replied, "but I think we are moving locations soon since we hired so many new people." That same co-worker had quit a few weeks later to work her dream job for a fashion magazine. Valerie had been an employee at SPRUCE for two years now, and they still had not moved office locations, and since no one

2

else had decorated their space, she never brought it up to her boss.

She spent a few hours after lunch making corrections to captions on posts. The amount of time she spent policing grammar was draining. She wanted to edit the photos at least; it killed her that she could not capture them. When one photographer, Chloe, decided to be a stay-at-home mother, Valerie had gotten her hopes up about finally being moved up to the position, but they hired Melissa instead. Matt attributed this to Valerie being "instrumental" to the company where she was. Flattering, but Valerie was still upset about it, and she tried not to compare herself to Melissa – who looked like she walked right out of a Cosmo magazine.

Valerie herself was not unattractive. She had an alternative style. Her wavy hair had a peek-a-boo dye job. The top was black, but underneath was bright teal, and it was chopped just above her shoulders. She had a 70's style fringe thing going on with her bangs and one small thin braid that was always in place behind her right ear. And she was curvy, but just a bit too curvy, where people stop saying curvy and start saying "bigger" in polite conversation as if to spare her feelings.

And she loved herself. But it was still hard not to wonder what it would be like to be Melissa and be able to find things that fit in any thrift store.

As if thinking about her had brought her into existence, Melissa knocked on Valerie's door. "Matt called a meeting."

"Thanks, be right there."

They met in the conference room. The conference room was a generous title for what was just a tiny room crammed with a too-large table where everyone had to struggle into their chairs. If the first people to arrive sat in the front of the room, then no one would be able to squeeze past them to the back side of the table. In short, this room was a nightmare. Valerie always tried to be one of the last people to arrive for any meetings in this room so she could slide into one of the convenient seats at the front. Sometimes she worried that people would notice her being late, but she would rather be known for being last to arrive than give everyone a show of her struggling from not being able to fit further back in the room. Especially when someone half her size couldn't fit easily.

"I have some very exciting news!" Steven from HR called the meeting to a start. "SPRUCE is expanding out of Washington to the sunny coast of Southern California!"

Co-workers began clapping. Matt and Steven were ping-ponging the presentation. Valerie tried to pay attention, but she was also working on generating hashtags for different types of accounts. "We have signed on a community theatre company in Oceanside, and Jorge will be going to build the account. Meanwhile, the finance department and management will set up an office space soon."

"There's an office already?" asked Elise, prone to blurting out questions during presentations.

"No, we are going to be shopping for one. But that's all behind the scenes. It's all going to come together," Matt replied.

Steven went on to explain that no one would be forced to relocate permanently, but if anyone was interested, to email him and they could discuss the possibility. "I can't make any promises though. It's my understanding that we would want to hire locals from the area. Keep an authentic feel in our product."

The weather in Seattle was cloudy on Valerie's drive home, but at least it wasn't raining. She hated the rain, hated how it made the lights on the street echo, hated how the windshield wipers were always either too fast or too slow, hated the feeling of water in her shoe, or a stray drop of rain sliding down her back. Thankfully, today she made her way to Tacoma without incident. The roads were clear, the ground did not reflect the lights, and her shoes remained dry until she made her way inside her apartment.

"Honey, I'm home!" she announced, flopping down on the couch. Out of the bedroom came a beautiful woman. This was Stacy Hadden, Valerie's long-term girlfriend.

"I'm actually just heading out," Stacy said.

"You are?" Valerie sat up and saw that Stacy was wearing her work clothes. As a bartender at The Last Bar, Stacy's work uniform was all black. A black T-shirt, black leggings, and black Doc Martens. The only thing that distinguished this as a work outfit was her name tag, which was shaped like a bottle of Jack Daniels on its side.

"I didn't know you had a shift. Isn't tonight date night?"

Stacy was looking in the mirror by the door, putting her chestnut hair up in a high ponytail, "Yeah, but I'm covering for Tammi." She came over and kissed Valerie on the cheek, "I'm closing, but I'll be home in the morning." Then as she walked through the front door, she called over her shoulder, "Bye!"

Valerie sank into the couch with an arm over her eyes. This was the third time in a row Stacy had canceled date night without talking about it with her first. Which was fine, she supposed. Stacy liked working because the tips were good. That was all. But for some reason, her last few paychecks hadn't been as much as they expected. "They started making us split our tips," she had said.

But Valerie knew all too well that Stacy had a history of being dishonest with romantic partners, and there was that lingering sense that something wasn't right.

Valerie and Stacy had been seeing each other for three months before she found out about Jessica. Jessica had messaged Valerie on Instagram. "I'm giving you the benefit of the doubt and assuming you didn't already know, but Stacy is a cheater. I just broke up with her. I don't want you to be blindsided like I was." As it turned out, Valerie was blindsided quite a bit. But Stacy had explained that Jessica was controlling, and

5

manipulative. Valerie wanted to make things work. Then Stacy moved in since Jessica had kicked her out.

The last two months though, Stacy has been staying out more. Valerie has felt more like a roommate than a girlfriend. Every time they tried to plan a romantic evening or prioritize some alone time, Stacy would take off. There was less intimacy. Not just physically, but Valerie felt like they didn't really talk about anything anymore, not like they did when they had first started dating. Back then, everything was urgent, every touch and kiss felt stolen, as if they would run out of time. Maybe that was the problem? Maybe passion was finite and they used it all up too fast. Did every relationship go this way?

And what was worse, was Valerie stopped fighting. She felt that fork in the road coming, where two people in a relationship go separate ways. She tried to hit the brakes, but the split was imminent. She wondered if Stacy saw it coming too. Thoughts of where Stacy was going and who she might be with flooded Valerie's brain.

Ding ding.

Valerie tried not to think about where Stacy might be going, and who she might be with. Her phone screen showed an email from Matt.

"Had a new client sign up for a full profile build, located in Southern California. Jorge was assigned but he got Covid, so he needs to quarantine. Can you take over? Need to be on-site the day after tomorrow."

Valerie jumped up to her feet so fast, she knocked over a throw pillow. Her initial instinct was to say "Yes, I will start packing," but she had to check with Stacy first. She was not a hypocrite after all, and for all she knew, Stacy may not feel the impending fork in the road. Stacy might think everything was fine. So, Valerie grabbed her keys and ran to her car without a care for the rain that had started to pour down around her.

Chapter 2

On an Oceanside beach, a woman with curly red hair wrapped up in a bun in a black bikini rolled over on her towel with her tattered copy of *An Actor Prepares*. She pulled her knees up to keep most of her hourglass frame in the shade of her umbrella.

"Amelia, you know I love you, but you are supposed to be *relaxing*. Not obsessing," said the black man next to her. He sat up and handed her the sunscreen. "You're burning, bestie."

She took the sunscreen and applied it to her legs. "I am not *obsessing*; I am just doing some light reading."

"About theatre stuff. You should listen to a podcast at least. Podcasts are so popular, there's a podcast for everything."

"Mostly murder," Amelia countered with a wrinkle of her nose.

"And mythology and some are stories or analyzing current events."

"But mostly crime." Amelia reiterated. The man beside her rolled his eyes dramatically and Amelia caved. "But I got the message, Jason." She put her book in her canvas bag. "Hand me some of those zucchini fries."

They watched some kids run in and out of the water as the waves stretched out along the sand and then retreated.

"I think we really needed this." Amelia mused. "I know it must have been hard seeing Austin at rehearsals."

Jason stiffened slightly at this but brushed it aside. "It's always awkward around an ex, but life goes on."

Amelia got the feeling that he was hiding his feelings, which was common for him. "Jason Rinehart, you shouldn't be bottling up all these emotions."

"Said the queen of emotional walls." Jason teased.

"Not with you," Amelia countered. "We have known each other far too long to start hiding things from each other."

"Ten years and counting," Jason waggled his thumb and pinkie in a *hang ten* gesture. Amelia raised her eyebrows as an invitation. "I am good, really. Am I super giddy about the fact that he's got a showmance growing with Emily? No. They can't help that they have that suggestive scene in "Moments in the Woods". But I am a big boy, I will deal."

Amelia thought back to six months ago when Jason had been crying on her bathroom floor after overindulging in the whiskey. He had been heartbroken when Austin ended things. "Is there anything I can do to make you more comfortable?" Amelia asked.

"Not a thing. He's the perfect choice for Cinderella's Prince. A total dick." Jason shook his head. "I just wish he could…" his voice trailed off. Amelia held his hand.

"I know, but you'll find the right person for you. That person is not Austin, as we learned the hard way, and that's his loss." Amelia squeezed Jason's hand. Jason squeezed back. "It's going to be you and me until we are old. Then we can let the aliens beam us up so we can die in space together."

"You and me, among the stars." Then they laughed until they noticed the wind had blown a napkin down the beach and seagulls were starting to fight over it. Jason ran them off while Amelia scooped up the napkin shreds that the birds left behind.

They made their way back to Jason's house, where he lived with his eccentric Aunt Kennedy, who at this time was traveling abroad in Denmark for the summer. Aunt Kennedy felt like an aunt to Amelia too. They would spend summers on the porch with matching frozen fruit popsicles, braids, and smiles clad in braces. This was the house where they got ready for prom together before their dates picked them up. This was also where Amelia hosted a superhero-themed coming-out party to kick off Jason's transition. It held so many memories, it felt like more of a home to her than her mom's house did.

The house had two bedrooms and two bathrooms and a two-car garage. Both bedrooms were upstairs. Aunt Kennedy's room was the larger of the two and was above the kitchen. Jason's room was smaller and was located above the garage. Between the rooms was one of the bathrooms, the only one with a bathtub. The guest bathroom was under the stairs.

"Shower time!" Jason hollered as he tossed Amelia a sea foam green bath towel. "I've decided that I am ordering us some sushi, we are going to celebrate!"

Amelia laughed, "What are we celebrating again?"

"That you are a kick ass director and that *Into the Woods* is going to be super fucking successful, duh!"

They laughed together.

"It had better be, especially since my loving family are so sure it'll flop, as if I don't know how to sell a show."

"Glen is such a persistent prick." Jason shook his head. "He cannot help but meddle in other people's business; however, I am glad that once the grand opening is done you'll have a little less weighing you down. Because you need to get back out on the field."

Amelia turned on her heel. "Shower time, remember?"

"Hey, I am just saying!" Jason hopped up the stairs as Amelia closed the door to the downstairs bathroom.

She knew that Jason meant well. She had a lot on her plate, but it didn't matter how much she delegated, this was her passion project. She was going to be the one to shoulder most of it. That was fine.

It was separate from the prospect of breaking down the walls that she had built to protect her heart. The shower's warm water ran down her body like little rivers as she washed the salty sand out of her hair. She tried to imagine the anxieties flowing down the drain.

Amelia was under a lot of stress, but for good reason. Those were the anxieties she was comfortable with. She was in the middle of launching a community theatre company as the world was slowly coming out of the thick of a global pandemic. That was bound to have a lot of triggers for her anxiety. Those triggers were manageable; she liked being able to point at the trigger and say, "That would stress anyone out." Then she could move on and tackle the issues.

But there were some fears that were illogical.

Like the fear of not being loveable in a romantic way.

Amelia got out of the shower and held eye contact with her reflection. As she looked at herself in the mirror. "You have no reason to think that you are unworthy of love," she told her reflection. Then she shifted uncomfortably to practice the affirmations that her therapist had given her.

"I am capable. I am competent. My existence is worthy of meaning just by being." Amelia stood there for a minute taking in her appearance as she waited for some kind of transformative mental breakthrough. She repeated the affirmations twice more.

Her fair ivory skin was slightly pink on the shoulders from the sun. Amelia shook her head, got dressed, and walked back out to the living room.

The white tile flooring was cool and smooth on her feet. Jason was sitting on the mauve couch with a to-go bag from Jade Sushi.

Amelia's stomach grumbled.

"This is the life," Jason said, popping his straw into his soda. Amelia nodded as she ate her veggie tempura. "Oh," he continued, "you left your phone out here, Luke called you."

"Ew, why?" Amelia groaned as she reached for her phone.

Jason shrugged.

Amelia settled on the couch cross-legged and called Luke back. "I'm annoyed that he can never just leave a voicemail," she said as the phone rang.

"Hey sis," Luke's deep voice came through the receiver. "How's it going?"

"Fine. You're on speaker. I'm with Jason; what's up?" Amelia rolled her eyes at Jason who nodded in understanding.

Luke was Amelia's older brother, seven years older. Amelia loved him, of course, but he was a little overbearing and a lot evasive in conversation.

"Well, I am really proud of you and Jason and opening this theatre."

"It's all her, man," Jason piped in.

Luke laughed, "Well I know that you are dead set on this, and it's admirable, really it is. But, you know, some part of me wants to agree with Uncle Glen and wishes you were doing something more reliable." There it was, once again. The undertones of disappointment with declarations of doubt. "So, here's the deal, if this proves to be unsuccessful, you drop it all and come work for us. Uncle Glen and I have really expanded the company since you were last here. It doesn't have to be medical billing, but you were good at it."

Amelia felt her stomach drop. Luke worked for their uncle's prestigious insurance company. When their dad left for his secret second family when she was a toddler, Uncle Glen financially supported them. Her mother's brother took Luke in under his wing, and now they were running the company their great-grandfather started. Luke had offered her a job before, and she had done it for a while, but the office life wasn't meant for her.

Still, she knew that this was meant to be a kindness. He was offering her a safety net and that there were so many people who would not have that luxury.

"Thanks, but I think it'll be okay."

"Ames, you're stubborn as hell, you know that?" he teased, but Amelia could hear the smile in his voice. "Evidence suggests that marketing for theatrical productions is more important than some other business models," Luke continued, "Purely because everything is so short term, a show plays for a month but only on weekends… it's not a lot of time for consumers to buy in."

Amelia and Jason looked at each other and waited for Luke to get to the point.

"So, I took the liberty of convincing Uncle to hire a marketing expert to handle that side of it for you."

"You what?" Amelia exclaimed. She didn't trust some stranger to advertise her show, she would rather trust a teenager to give her a tattoo. It was one of those things that she felt strongly about. "Why would you do that? Why would you take that from me?" she felt her chest squeeze, felt the familiar claws of anxiety digging into her throat as it tried to pull itself out.

Amelia tried to swallow.

"I'm not taking anything!" Luke retorted, his exasperation evident. "I managed to appease Uncle Glen with the crack deal of you getting a fair shot before he went out there to shut you guys down."

"Could he do that?" Jason asked.

"Never underestimate an old man with deep pockets and the audacity," Luke replied. "The marketing agent is supposed to be there sometime this week. I think his name is Jorge." There was a sound of someone in the background calling out to Luke. "Hey, Amelia, it's going to be okay. I'm in your corner. I need to go, we'll talk later."

Amelia looked at her phone as it went back to her home screen.

"I cannot fucking believe it." Amelia hissed. Jason just shrugged noncommittally. "What's that supposed to mean?"

"Just… it's nice that you'll have one less thing to worry about," Jason said sheepishly. "You would run yourself into the ground and dig yourself an early grave if no one took away some of your shovels."

"That doesn't even make sense," Amelia deflected.

"Yes, it did. You know what I mean. Here, have another bite of sushi."

Amelia got up and started pacing. "I haven't even told you my pitch yet."

"What pitch?" asked Jason nervously.

Amelia stopped pacing and clasped her hands in front of her, an air of a formal professional businesswoman. "You know how my roommates have officially moved out?"

"Right, because they lost their jobs during the pandemic and haven't gone back to work yet," Jason replied. "Which, honestly, I believe that Toni could not find new work because she's an anti-vax nurse –"

"A fucking oxymoron."

"But Sam? She just did not want to work. She could have bartended anywhere or gotten some form of income." Jason rotated a hand in emphasis.

"Sam just hated working."

"And I hate her." Jason snipped.

"I know you do, but back to the point," Amelia redirected. "I have an empty bedroom in my apartment that costs an arm and a leg for rent and currently, I only have one leg to stand on. I was wondering… if you would consider moving in?"

"Bestie," Jason started.

"You'd have your own room." Amelia pitched.

"I have my own room." Strike one.

"You'll have the bigger of the two rooms," she tried again.

"I don't pay rent here." Strike two.

"You would get to live with me?" A final plea.

Jason stood up and took Amelia's hands. "Babe, I love you. But I cannot afford an apartment, even half of an apartment. I have medical bills to pay for. Have you asked anyone else?"

They sat back down on the couch. "I don't feel comfortable living with anyone else right now. But I have picked up some extra shifts at the coffee shop tomorrow."

"Hey! That's good news!" Jason lifted his sparkling water in cheers. Amelia clinked her can with his halfheartedly.

"I have enough cash to survive two months, but depending on how the show opens in a few weeks, I may start looking for a smaller apartment," Amelia said.

Jason held her hand again. "It is going to be alright."

Chapter 3

The Last Bar was a building on a street packed tight with thin, tall, decorative buildings. It was painted navy blue with golden accents. It was not a sports bar, but almost an academic style. The floors were black and white alternating tile, and the lights were Edison bulbs.

When Valerie walked in, sound poured out and enveloped her. The bar was not packed, but it was a Friday night. People were scattered about in groups. There was a group of middle-aged men drinking scotch in the booth by the door.

"I disagree," said one of the men, who stood up as Valerie walked in, blocking her path through the entryway, "The Socratic Method is a valuable tool to guide students through the material to their own conclusions. I feel like it's even more important now, in a generation of university students who do not want to *learn*, they just want to *know*. I feel as though it is our responsibility as their professors to foster an attitude of learning, not just route memorization."

"Sit down Jimmy, you are blocking the lady," said a man still sitting.

The one named Jimmy apologized and sat back down.

Valerie continued to the bar and grabbed a seat. The barstools were emerald green and the wall behind the bar was one long mirror which made it easy to see the whole room even when facing forward. She looked around, and with no sign yet of Stacy, she grabbed her phone to check the email again.

On-site the day after tomorrow. Southern California. Excitement swelled in her chest. Of course, Valerie was worried about Jorge and hoped that he recovered soon. But a whole profile build? She could hardly believe it.

Life had been feeling stagnant. Stuck. Like she was going to continue working in a job she did not hate but did not love. And maybe once her career started feeling better, maybe things with Stacy would feel better too.

"Hey, Valerie."

Valerie looked up; that wasn't Stacy's voice. "Oh, hey Janelle. Is Stacy around?"

Janelle shook her head.

"Oh, okay… Is she on a break or something?"

"It's her night off," Janelle said, drying a glass.

"Right, but she's covering for Tammi." Valerie tried again. "Look, it's really urgent I talk to her. I have really important news." *I don't want her to find out that I left the state without talking to her first.*

"I'm covering for Tammi," Janelle said and handed her a shot of tequila with lime. "Look, I try to stay out of people's business, but you're really nice and, well, I'd want to know." Janelle got a shot for herself too.

Valerie felt her stomach drop. She heard her blood pumping in her ears. She felt like there was a rubber band in her chest that had been pulled too tight; it snapped and rendered her numb.

"She said she would be here," Valerie repeated. "To cover Tammi. But you're here, covering for Tammi…" She felt like her brain was going ten times slower than normal. She took the shot of tequila and grimaced as she chased it down with a bite of lime. She felt like an idiot.

"Stacy and Tammi?" Valerie asked, needing to verify.

With a small nod, Janelle refilled her shot glass and then they each threw them back. As Valerie bit into the lime, she thought *So, we already passed the fork in the road.*

"How long?" she asked.

"I'm not sure," Janelle replied, although Valerie was unconvinced. "Does it make a difference?" Janelle looked at her- with sympathy or pity, she could not tell.

Just then, the doors opened and in came Stacy, Tammi, and a few others that Valerie did not recognize. It was like she was experiencing tunnel vision, watching as Stacy and Tammi

15

had their arms around each other as they stumbled their way through the bar. Valerie felt herself stiffen.

The group had funneled into a booth behind her across the room. Valerie could see them over her shoulder through the mirror behind the bar. She kept her eyes forward.

"You good? I don't want any trouble on my shift." Janelle asked as if she was worried that Valerie would get up and start an old-fashioned brawl.

"Don't worry, I'm not a fighter."

Through the mirror, Valerie watched as Stacy leaned in and started to make out with Tammi. Gritting her teeth, Valerie grabbed her wallet to pay for the shot and leave. Janelle shook her head. "It's on the house."

Valerie rose to leave, determined to walk right out the door, but of course, as she stood in the threshold she looked back. Stacy and Tammi weren't even looking her way. It was as if she didn't exist.

When she arrived home, she brewed a large thermos of coffee. While she paced in the small kitchen, she called her boss.

"Hey Matt, I thought it'd be faster to call," she said. "I'm happy to help. Can you send me the address?"

Matt had explained to her that they had a flight from Seattle to San Diego taking off in the morning, but Valerie insisted on driving.

"It's already paid for," Matt insisted on the phone. "And non-refundable."

"I don't know how else to say this; I am not getting on a plane." Valerie packed her bag by throwing all the clothes she would need on top of her duffle bag and stuffing them in when it came time to zip it up.

"Fine, we'll try to adjust it somehow. We can transfer it or change the date or flight. This is a big opportunity. This is our first client outside of the Pacific Northwest, which could mean big things for our company overall."

Valerie shoved her phone into her back pocket and looked around the apartment. She had her clothes, her work bag, and photography equipment. She locked the doors and loaded her luggage into her car. Before she left, she confirmed that Matt had sent her information and the client's folder through her email.

"It's a good thing I got an oil change last week," she said to her car or to no one. The car purred to life and as soon as her Bluetooth connected, she turned on a road trip playlist. She got on the I-5 and started driving south.

About ten minutes into the drive, Stacy had called her. Valerie declined the call. Then she called again. And again. Valerie ended up turning her phone off, trading her playlist for the one Taylor Swift CD in her car.

It was already midnight when she rolled through the Washington-Oregon border and decided to pull over and sleep.

Up in her hotel room, she plugged her phone into the charger and as it turned on, it lit up with a ton of messages from Stacy. Valerie sighed and opened the text conversation.

     S: *Babe, what is going on?*

     S: *I think I saw you leave the bar. Why were you talking to Janelle? And drinking with her?*

     S: *Babe, please.*

     S: *Why aren't you picking up?*

     S: *I am heading home now.*

     S: *Where are you? Your location is turned off. I am freaking out. Please, at least tell me you are safe.*

     S: *Valerie. Pick. Up.*

     S: *It's been a few hours. I get that you are upset, and honestly, I do not know what Janelle told you, but this is fucked up.*

Just then, another message popped up.

S: *Wow, you are just going to read my messages
and not reply? When I've been worried about you? Ghosting me
and leaving me on read? Is that where our relationship is
headed?*

Valerie rolled her eyes and called; she did not have the
energy to deal with the rapid assault of text messages.

"Hey," Stacy said when she picked up the phone.
"Hey," Valerie replied. The silence hung in the air;
Valerie swore she could feel the weight of her disappointment in
her phone. "I'm sorry you were worried."
"Yeah, it's pretty fucked up that you would just take off
like that." Stacy's indignation was sharp and cutting.
"It was more fucked up to find out that you've been
cheating on me, but that's all nuance I guess," Valerie feigned a
sneer.
"Are you going to tell me where you are?" Stacy asked
in a way that was more of a demand than a request.
"Are you even going to deny it, Stacy?"
The inhale of frustration could be heard through the
receiver. "Deny what, Valerie?"
"That you are cheating on me!" Valerie exploded. "With
Tammi. That you lied to me about having work tonight. That
you've probably been doing this for a while and playing me for a
fucking fool! I don't know how I missed it. You were working
all this 'overtime' and yet your paychecks were consistently
less."
"You know what Valerie; this is exactly why I had to lie
to you. I was not cheating on you. It was her birthday. And she
wanted to have a get-together and go to a club and I knew you'd
be like this, so I did not tell you."
Valerie took a deep breath that was meant to be calming
but just made her sound more agitated. "Stacy, when have I ever
cared if you went out with your friends?"

18

"You're doing it right now."

"I literally saw you. And Janelle told me ..." Valerie started.

"Well, Janelle needs to mind her own fucking business." Stacy cut her off. "You really don't believe me? When have I ever given you a reason to think I would be unfaithful to you?"

Flabbergasted, Valerie could not even add venom to her response. "When I found out I was the other woman from your last relationship."

"Oh my god; you're seriously bringing that up? Now?" Valerie held her breath. "You know what, fuck this. I have shit to do. You can believe what you want. I'm not going to play this fucking game."

"Stacy, I am gone for work," Valerie made sure to enunciate each word, trying to keep her volume and tone level, "I will be back in a month," Valerie said. "I want you gone when I am home. You have plenty of time to find a new place."

"Fuck you," Stacy said and then hung up.

Valerie gave in to exhaustion and crawled under the covers. Confrontation had never been her strength. The blow-up with Stacy had drained her of all her remaining energy. She decided to just take the rest while she could. She would be driving the majority of the next day.

Chapter 4

Sleep was elusive. Regardless, morning came, and Valerie grabbed her suitcase and got back on the road; there was still a lot of ground to cover. California was huge. Once she had broken free of the tree line, there was so much openness. Fields of agriculture, desert stretches, and eventually, the coast keeping her company on the passenger side. It was the same ocean that she knew from home, but it seemed different already.

Maybe it was the sunshine, maybe it was the traffic, or maybe it was the fact that she was suddenly freshly single.

Valerie felt adamant that she had made the right call. If she was being honest with herself, she was not even sad about the breakup. Not in a way that was significant. It was upsetting, but not debilitating. Rather the opposite. It was almost… liberating.

Being in a relationship with Stacy was like being in a small room with a viper. Quick to the defensive, Valerie had developed the habit of always looking for the hidden knife. Stacy was the kind to shoot first and ask questions later. There had been a lot of little things that would end up in a full-blown fight.

Valerie should've known from the first time they fought, and Stacy said that makeup sex was her favorite.

And Stacy knew that no one could make up if they do not have a fight first.

Valerie felt like she had been living in a constant state of fight or flight for the last several months and knowing that she had physical distance from the drama for at least the next few weeks felt like a deep breath.

When she arrived at the hotel in Oceanside, she found that Jorge or Matt had already splurged SPRUCE money on a room with a view of the ocean. The sun had just set, but it was still dusk. "Gorgeous," Valerie said aloud.

Her stomach rumbled in response.

Valerie walked to a café down Pacific Coast Highway, relishing the fact that she was able to walk down the road in the early evening and not need a jacket or umbrella.

The café was cute, with some large faux leather couches in the middle of the room facing each other with a low table in between. The wall facing the Pacific Coast Highway was made entirely of windows. The window wall had evenly spaced two-person round tables. Towards the back were a few four-person square tables that each had people, mostly with laptops.

Valerie opted for a chair and table by the window so she could look outside. The Rose Theatre, her client, was located across the street. She studied it while waiting for her order.

It was the best veggie panini she had ever eaten; the hummus made all the difference.

"Need a refill?" the barista asked.

Valerie nodded. "Yeah, thanks. Hey, what can you tell me about that theatre?" She might as well try and get a sample of the local interest level and try and gauge how much marketing she needed to do.

"Oh, it was just reopened. There's going to be a show in a few weeks," the barista replied. She had copper hair and fair skin, not quite ivory, but not quite tanned. Valerie broke concentration on the building, distracted by the beauty before her.

"Are you going to go see it?" Valerie asked.

"Oh, absolutely. You should too," the barista replied with a coy smile.

Valerie smiled. That was too vague to be an invitation, but maybe it could be.

"I am actually here to help with the marketing, so I will be seeing it a few times, I'm sure."

The barista's eyebrows lifted slightly. "Is that right?" The barista was looking at her as if she couldn't decide if Valerie was a friend or foe.

Valerie could not tell what was causing this shift in energy. Had she said something wrong? Maybe she was still in shock over finally ending things with Stacy that she was off her game. Or maybe she never had game. Who was she to say?

At the thought of Stacy, two conflicting emotions arose. On the one hand, she could cry and feel bad because she had been cheated on. Or, on the other hand, she could move on and have a good time because she was single and in California.

The latter was more appealing.

"I work for this company in the SeaTac area," Valerie said, feeling like her foot was in her mouth, but unsure as to why or how to get it out. "Helping businesses create and maintain a social media presence." *Why am I giving a sales pitch?*

The barista remained silent, and Valerie felt awkward, so she just kept talking. "I mean, I hope they let me do my job. The guy who hired me actually doesn't own the business but he has his own ideas. It gets tricky because he's the client and we want to make the client happy, obviously, but I hope the business owner has the same vision. That normally doesn't happen."

The barista shrugged as she turned to put the coffee pot back on the counter. "Well, as long as you do your job and work respectfully, I do not think you'll have any issues with her," the barista said, taking off her apron and tucking it on a shelf behind the counter.

Valerie perked up, "Oh, do you know the owner? Maybe you can give me some insight?" then because she did not feel like she could embarrass herself more, "Maybe tonight? Over dinner?"

The barista let out a light laugh. "I would, but I have rehearsal. My name is Amelia, I am the owner and creative director at the Rose Theatre. A pleasure to meet you…"

Amelia held out her hand, as she spoke Valerie felt her face warm and heard the blood pounding in her ears.

"Uh, hi! I am Valerie!" she said, too loudly. *What the hell is wrong with you?* She thought as she took Amelia's hand

and shook it. They looked at each other, Valerie tried to say something else as the silence stretched between them like a dark void. She realized that she was holding Amelia's hand a little too long and let go with a start.

"Well, I'll see you tomorrow. Does 10 A.M. work?" she asked.

"Tomorrow?" Valerie asked, her head still swimming in her own embarrassment, resisting the urge to wipe her clammy hand on the thigh of her pants.

"For an initial meeting?" Amelia said in that patient, but irritated tone teachers use when they remind students to put their names on their homework for the twentieth time.

"Oh, yes, yes!" Valerie's face felt so warm, she could only hope that her blush was subtle. Amelia took off her apron and tossed it into a laundry basket behind the counter. "I'm off, Mel," she called to a co-worker in the back before turning back to Valerie. "I'll see you then," she said in farewell and walked out of the coffee shop across the street to the theatre.

Valerie watched her go as she finished her raspberry mocha latte. Amelia's red hair in the light was out of this world. *I can't believe I tried to flirt with a client like that,* she thought, *and it wasn't even good flirting! What the fuck, Valerie.*

When Amelia got to the theatre Jason was already waiting for her.

"Hey bestie," he said, "how was the day job?"

"It was… fine." Amelia said.

"Did something happen?" Jason asked. "You're being weird."

"I met our marketing liaison," Amelia didn't look at Jason as she spoke. She focused on preparing her notebook and water bottle to keep her hands busy. "I'm meeting her officially tomorrow."

"Oof, was it weird?"

"Um, no." Amelia bit her lip a bit. "She's cute."

Jason spread his hands to signify a need for a stop. "Did you just say she was cute? After not dating in two years?"

"Okay, it's not that big of a deal."

"It *is* a big deal. I thought you were turning into a nun or something. Saving yourself for the theatre gods." Jason feigned fanning himself. "And all it took was for you to need to collaborate with someone potentially."

"She asked me out," Amelia admitted, "She didn't know I was the owner, just a barista."

"Okay, what did you say?"

"I told her I had rehearsal."

Jason facepalmed. "Your game is weak, girl."

At that moment, some of the cast members started walking in. "It doesn't matter. I don't want to just jump into bed with her, you know?"

"No, I don't."

"I need to work with her!" Jason waved his hand as if to ask her what the point is. "So, I need to maintain a professional relationship."

"Uh huh," Jason said. "But you think she's cute?"

Amelia kept her mouth shut but couldn't keep the color rising in her cheeks.

Chapter 5

The next day, Amelia grabbed a latte from the café at 9:45 A.M. She did not want to be late for her first official meeting with Valerie.

All night she had thought about the conversation they had. It was crazy. She didn't know this woman. She was supposed to not like her, she was an instrument that her meddling brother and uncle were using because they didn't believe that she could open a theatre on her own.

But Valerie didn't know that. She was just doing her job. So, Amelia wanted to let her guard down until she knew she needed them.

Valerie was waiting outside in some black business pants and a royal blue button-up. She looked amazing, not that Amelia noticed, of course.

Amelia crossed the street and handed Valerie a hot coffee-to-go cup.

"Raspberry mocha?" she asked.

Valerie smiled, "Oh my god, thank you! The coffee at the hotel was so gross. I couldn't force myself to drink it. What do I owe you?"

Amelia waved her offer away with a flick of her hand. "Don't worry about it."

She unlocked the glass door into the lobby. "I have already had a lot of the remodeling work done," she said. The lobby walls were a muted grey-blue, and the ceiling was painted to look like a night sky, with constellations named and outlined.

"Eventually I will get new flooring. Anyway, let's go to the office." A few of the light grey tiles in the lobby were

25

cracked, but not so bad. The once black carpet that Amelia was walking on toward the office however needed replacing. It was so worn down; you could see the years of foot traffic.

Amelia opened another door to the office. There was a single desk with two standard guest chairs and a long conference table. Amelia sat at the table, so Valerie followed suit.

"Okay, so run me through this."

"Well," Valerie said, pulling up the file on her phone, "it says here you bought this building in cash, which had been a community theatre before the pandemic."

"Yep,"

"Part of what I want to do here is highlight the history of this building, along with your personal history. With local businesses like this, putting a name, face, and story to a place really helps community involvement."

"Okay. So, what else do you need to know? I believe my uncle told Jorge already about the building and its history, and an internet search is easy to do."

"You're right, he did, and Jorge forwarded those emails to me, so I have them. I guess I am asking for your story, with the building or the community. From your perspective, not your uncle's. Why you chose to open a theatre and why now?"

Amelia thought for a moment, her arms crossed, and leaned back in her chair with her face towards the ceiling.

"It's only in the theatre I ever lived." She said after a while. "That's a quote by the way. Wilde. And it really resonates with me. I found myself the first time I was in theatre. Theatre is an art. People forget that sometimes. I think because of the performance element, there is some kind of stigma or illusion that only professionals can do theatre, but that's not true."

"So do you see a lot of people wanting to be professionals or the opposite?" Valerie asked.

"I mean, yes. A lot of people want to be famous for acting in movies and television, but why should only the lucky few get to act? It's like, imagine if someone was gatekeeping painting. It's crazy to be in that mindset of 'Well, I'm not Van Gough so I can never ever paint anything.' Why does the love of a craft mean you have to make it your whole career?"

"Did you ever want to be famous?" Valerie asked, more for herself than for the interview.

Amelia shook her head, "This is the big time right here. Bringing people together, making theatre accessible for audiences and theatre artists alike. That's the whole point."

Valerie wished she could take her camera out and take a picture of Amelia right now and the way she was practically glowing as she talked about the theatre. "That would be a great caption," she said instead. "How does this philosophy feed into or lend itself to the process of deciding which shows you want to put on?"

Amelia adjusted in her seat. "Well, there's a lot that goes into that. You can't just pick a show that's popular to fill seats, and you can't just pick shows that are cheap to produce because it might be a complete flop. I prefer stories that mean something. I think that as long as there's a message to send or a lesson to learn, then I'm game. And the coolest part is that every story matters. Even shows that on the surface seem whimsical or silly have something that will resonate with audiences."

"So why start a theatre now?"

"The pandemic was really hard, for a lot of people and a lot of industries. And the arts were no exception. It's hard to go from doing what you love to being labeled 'non-essential'." Amelia debated stopping there, but she felt like she could be open with Valerie. "Off the record, I was living with my ex, and she's a Corpsman, which basically means a nurse in the Navy but her patients are Marines. Anyway, long story short, we broke up." Amelia shakes her head and adjusts, "That... that's not important. For the record, I had to figure out a way to support myself. I ended up getting an associate degree and a career in medical billing, started working... and I hated it. I looked at my savings and my options and I got a business loan and opened The Rose Theatre. I quit my medical billing job and I haven't looked back. I put all my eggs in this basket, and I am doing everything I can to not drop it."

Valerie looked down at her notepad, but she wasn't writing. Amelia wondered if she had said the wrong thing or not enough. Valerie looked puzzled.

"And you just… did the thing," she said finally, a strange tone in her voice.

Amelia took a second, looked around, and her smile spread itself like butter.

"Yeah, I did. I can give you a tour?" she offered.

"Yes, absolutely," Valerie stood up to follow her.

The lobby branched off in two directions that wrapped around and opened into the audience seating area. The building had been a single-screen movie theatre once.

"These are the original seats!" Amelia exclaimed. "I restuffed them; ninety-nine seats exactly. I did have to reupholster a few but I got a maroon velvet that matches perfectly."

They walked up the steps to the back where there was a makeshift tech booth. Valerie took in the information as Amelia explained the sound board, light board, and the wiring she had set up with Jason.

"It's one of those things that you have to really do well the first time, so it's adjustable for whatever any future show needs," Amelia explained.

"Is Jason a business partner?" Valerie asked.

"Basically. He doesn't have the same stake in the financial side of it, but he definitely has an equal share of sweat equity."

Behind the booth were two rooms. One had a plexiglass wall that had a square cut out for a spotlight. "This is a manually operated spotlight. This room used to be for nursing mothers to be able to watch movies but still have privacy. Now it's storage for cables and mic packs."

The other door went up a few steps. "This is like a tech break room. It used to be the camera room for the movies." The room had a couch, a mini fridge, a coffee maker, and a workbench with an old soundboard and a source four light on it. There were two armchairs with a small table between them on the opposite side of the room from the door. The walls were decorated with movie posters and Christmas lights.

28

"I picture coming in here for intermissions or to hang out before shows. There's a bathroom too, which will be useful if anyone in the booth needs to use the restroom during a show, we will not have to walk all the way through the audience to the lobby and back."

"Very practical," Valerie agreed. She could see that Amelia was proud of this place, as she should be. It was a huge feat to open a business at all, let alone in a building as large as this. Valerie wondered how substantial of a business loan she had taken out.

Amelia led Valerie back down the steps to the stage. "This is the scrim, which we use for projections, but behind it…" Amelia showed Valerie a black wall. "I thought about raising the scrim and projecting on here directly. If it was painted as well, it could be a cool mixed media set." They walked around to the back, where there were a few "dressing rooms" constructed out of flats, 2x4s, and shower curtains. "These are going to be for leads or characters with a lot of quick changes." Across from the dressing rooms were a few couches, chairs, and tables stacked on top of each other to make room for a clear walkway. There was also a caged-off area that had power and hand tools on the walls. There was a padlock on the door. "Better to be safe than sorry. I don't want anyone messing around with power tools and accidentally losing a finger," Amelia explained.

Following the walkway down another set of stairs was a door that was held ajar by a traffic cone. This little gated outdoor area was big enough to park two cars, but there were no cars, just a few flats made out to be a forest scene and some spray paint cans.

Taking a hard left through another door, Amelia and Valerie were in a mirrored room with hard flooring. "This is where we have dance rehearsals, obviously," Amelia gestured to the wall of mirrors.

"This is incredible," Valerie said. Amelia had a full floor plan designed for her needs already, and she hadn't even opened her first show.

"I am really fortunate," Amelia beamed. They continued with the tour. There was another room attached in a type of alcove or large closet that was a traditional dressing room with big light bulbs surrounding mirrors above a counter that ran the length of a wall. "We don't have gendered dressing rooms. Each changing area is an individual stall. It's more trans and non-binary inclusive that way."

Adjacent to the mirrors were more of the handmade changing rooms with miscellaneous curtains. One curtain had little yellow stars on a dark blue background, another was white with watercolor oranges on it, a third had an underwater scene on it, including an orca and a pod of dolphins.

"This is where the costume loft is," Amelia gestured to another door, this one with a narrow mirror hanging from the top of it. "The previous owners donated all their costumes when I bought the building. But we don't have to go up all those steps right now."

"This is really cool," Valerie said. "I am excited to help you make your dream successful."

Amelia paused. "Can I say something that might sound mean? I don't want it to be rude, I just can't think of another way to phrase it."

"Uh, sure?" Valerie said.

"I didn't want you here, and I'm still not entirely sure that having a marketing liaison is necessary."

Valerie opened her mouth, then shut it again. What could she say?

"I mean," Amelia went on, color rising in her cheeks, "I didn't ask for someone to take over marketing and I didn't agree to this when my brother and uncle hired SPRUCE. They didn't really give me a chance. And they told me it would be someone named Jorge, and instead, you're here."

"Oh, I… Jorge has Covid, so I was told to come down two days ago. I didn't know that you didn't know, and if you prefer Jorge," Valerie trailed off. She felt so stupid. She hadn't even had a chance to start working on this project, and already it was being taken from her.

"No, that's not what I mean," Amelia interjected. "I'm just… having you here makes me nervous." Then her blush reddened. "Because of the theatre," she hurried to say, "I've put my whole self into this place and it's hard to trust someone else with my baby. And I can never tell if my uncle wants me to succeed or fail and I just," a shaky breath left her. "I'm sorry, I'm just anxious."

Valerie wanted to take her hand, she was anxious too, but that wouldn't be very professional. "I get it," she said instead, "but I need you to know that I'm serious when I say that I want to help *you*. Not just because it's my job, but because I can see how much this is your passion and you, this place, your story… it's inspiring. This is going to be a asset to your community."

"I really want this to work out," Amelia said, "so I want us to work together on it. This theatre is like my baby, I'm trusting you with her face by trusting you with marketing."

"And I don't take that trust lightly," Valerie assured her.

Amelia grabbed a binder from the counter and handed it to her. "This is the book for the show. Please read it. You cannot promote a show unless you know it backward and forwards."

Valerie took the binder and took some notes on movie adaptations and recorded live performances to look up for context.

"Let me know if you have any questions about the thematical elements of the show," Amelia said as they left the theatre.

"Okay, thanks." Valerie put the binder in her bag. "I'll go read through this and do some research. What time would you like me on site?"

"We start at 7 P.M.," Amelia said.

"Sounds good, I'll see you tomorrow, Amelia," Valerie said.

"Tomorrow." Amelia agreed.

As Valerie left, Amelia went back to her apartment. It was too quiet and too big for her to live in alone. She wondered absently if she should get a pet as she put Lord of the Rings Ambiance on her television.

She took out her phone and made a video call to Jason.

"Wassup, bitch," he answered the phone.

"Nothing much, whore," she teased back.

"Did you meet with the marketing person?" Jason was lounging in his bed playing video games so his eyes were focused on the game. Still, Amelia preferred the video calls to the regular phone calls, even if they weren't looking at each other.

"I did. Her name is Valerie."

"Did she give you a business plan or whatever your uncle wanted her to do?" Jason's head reacted in a dodge to the fight he was playing in the game.

"No," Amelia thought back, "but she's nice. She was interested in what I had to say. I gave her a tour. She's nice… and pretty."

"Wait, hold on." Jason paused the game and picked up the phone. He made a big show of giving Amelia his full attention. "Are you going to shoot your shot?"

Amelia laughed. "We just met, Jason, God."

"Okay, and? She literally asked you out yesterday. As the kids say, the ball is in your court."

"Oh is that what the kids say?" Amelia laughed, "But to answer your question, I am more focused on how to get the show performance ready."

"Uh-huh." Jason gave her a knowing smirk.

"When are you going to hang lights at The Rose?" she asked.

"Nice deflection."

"I am not deflecting; I am asking an important question."

"Which you already know the answer to because you scheduled it." Jason shot back.

Amelia shook her head. "Whatever, I will talk to you later."

"Love you, bye."

"Love you, bye." She hung up.

Amelia looked around her apartment and decided that getting a pet would be too much additional responsibility, but plants would be nice. She didn't have time for dates right now. As enchanted as she was by the idea of Valerie, now was the time to buckle down and focus. Maybe also find a smaller place to live if she couldn't secure a roommate.

Chapter 6

Valerie was surprised at the amount of people involved in this production. *The larger the cast, the larger the immediate crowd,* Valerie thought. If each cast member had two people see the show, then word of mouth would do a lot of her job for her.

Amelia called everyone's attention. "Can everyone sit in the first three rows, please!" As everyone shuffled into their seats, Amelia gestured to Valerie as if to say, *you, here, with me.*

"First things first, I wanted to notify you guys that the dressing rooms are going to be open starting tonight, so we can get our bodies familiar with the distance for entrances. Next week I will want you guys in the dressing room whenever you are off-stage. We need to practice doing that so we do not end up having the whole cast in the wings when our crew is trying to execute scene changes. Alright?"

The cast nodded.

"Also, I would like to introduce you all to Valerie. She's going to be helping with the marketing for the show."

Valerie did an awkward wave at her name. Amelia was looking at her expectantly.

"Yeah, I will just be, uh, taking photos and videos and stuff. Behind the scenes and promotional stuff. It'll all be for the show, so it's good stuff." *Wow, how many times am I going to say "stuff"?* Valerie's cheeks warmed, and Amelia took the reins.

"Yes, it will be good. Go ahead and have a seat, Valerie." Valerie sat down and tried to calm her breathing, then she tried to ignore her breathing as if that would make it fix itself. "Valerie will not get in our way, in general, while you are rehearsing, I need you to act like she's an audience member, her camera is an audience member. Ignore them."

Valerie felt like that might be a bit far. Hopefully, she could have some involvement with the actors so she could highlight their personalities a bit; "ignore" was overcorrecting. She did not speak up against it though. She would just have to see what parameters she could work in.

"Tomorrow, Valerie will take some headshots. Make sure your hair and makeup are ready at the start of rehearsal so we can hammer those out. Wear black T-shirts. We want these headshots to be uniform for the program. We'll take character headshots later when we have the costumes figured out."

Rehearsal started soon after. Valerie had read the book over the weekend, but still hearing the complexity of the music was astounding. Amelia was sitting in the middle of the audience, and a young man was next to her with a big binder, a legal pad, and a clipboard. He was going back and forth between them all furiously, his eyes mostly on the papers.

However, Amelia had her eyes on the stage ninety-nine percent of the time, only occasionally looking down at her own small notebook. Most of the time, she seemed to write notes without looking. Valerie snapped a photo of the two of them. She could not help but notice how regal Amelia looked. The soft waves of her hair were emphasized by how she was using reading glasses to hold them up.

"Okay good!" she said. "I do not think we need to run that again today. Now, Cinderella, I would like to work on 'On the Steps of the Palace' with you."

A girl in her early twenties with a melancholic air about her, stood up. Her jet-black hair was pulled into a loose ponytail, and she was wearing burnt orange overalls with a lilac t-shirt underneath. Cinderella went on stage.

"Let's act it out speaking, then sing, then act and sing. Okay?" Amelia said.

Jason started the music. Valerie felt really connected to the lyrics, the indecision of Cinderella not knowing what to choose when it came to running from the ball or being caught by the prince. Valerie did not know if she should pursue Amelia or hurry through the job and get home; if she should take the leap and pursue her own dream.

"How did that feel?" Amelia asked Cinderella after running the number with blocking and singing.

"I feel a little weird about the shoe being stuck while I am trying to pull my foot out. Is there a way we can make it stick for real? I feel like I am moving my foot around a lot," Cinderella said.

Jason got his pencil ready to take notes on his rehearsal report. Valerie looked over and saw that it was a simple sheet that had different sections for notes relevant to props, lighting, sound, costuming, et cetera.

"It's not coming across like that at all. You're doing a great job, but how about this? Let's run the number again, and you can have free play with the blocking and maybe we can find a solution."

They ran the number again. Cinderella tried some different choices, and they concluded that she would take the shoe off earlier. Valerie was amazed at the collaboration and how effortless it seemed.

While Amelia was directing, Valerie let her mind wander. There was already a surprising amount of attraction that Valerie was feeling. She wondered what the human resources department would say about this. It was probably a clear "do not try to romance and/or seduce clients or any employees therein" policy. But technically, Amelia's uncle was the client, and he was not affiliated with the theatre in any professional aspect. Did that make Amelia more or less of a client? How far removed from the contractual business relationship could the argument be made? There was certainly a grey area if she looked for it. *The best option is probably to just not do anything*, she decided. She could not risk losing her job right now, not when she had the hope of becoming a full-time photographer – either with SPRUCE or on her own.

At the end of rehearsal, Amelia had the cast circle up as she gave some feedback. Valerie took photos of the process and watched as Jason scribbled down lists of costumes, props, set dressings, and other things that still needed to be made, found, or bought. As the cast was dismissed, Jason handed the list to Amelia.

"I have an appointment out of town tomorrow, so I can't go hunting for this stuff," he told her.

"I hate shopping by myself," Amelia said.

"Valerie," Jason said, as he noticed that she was the last one there. "What are you doing tomorrow?"

"Umm, not much. I have a bit of editing to do and some research."

"Perfect," Jason clapped his hands together and grabbed his backpack.

Amelia looked a bit annoyed. Valerie could not tell if it was annoyance at Jason or annoyance at the idea of hanging out with her.

"Let's meet at the library at nine?" Amelia offered.

"Sure," Valerie said. "If you want me to, I don't want to bother you."

Amelia smiled a small smile, "It's not a bother, I will be happy for the company, and I look forward to getting to know you a bit better."

Chapter 7

The library was small but comforting. There was reddish brown carpeting and dark wood shelves. There were cute hand-decorated chalkboard signs distinguishing genres. There were different displays set up. One for a job fair, one for a knitting circle book club combo, as well as flyers for an after-school program that helped students with their homework and provided pizza for dinner.

The library was empty, which was not surprising for a Tuesday morning. There was a homeless man at a computer filling out a job application, and a mother with two young boys in the children's section, which was just one corner of the library with some bookshelves arranged into a corral.

In the back, the library had an enclosed garden. There was a small water fountain that looked like rocks stacked on top of each other. Valerie saw Amelia sitting at a bistro table under an umbrella. She was wearing light-wash jeans and a dark green crop top. There were a few weed-like indigenous flowers too. Throughout the last few days, Valerie watched rehearsals and took some cast photos. They hadn't interacted much more than the occasional direction from Amelia to Valerie, but each day, she made sure Valerie was part of the circle at the end of rehearsal. It really made Valerie feel

"This place is really cute," Valerie said, as she slid into a chair opposite Amelia.

Amelia looked around as if she had never really looked before. "Yeah, it is. I like the atmosphere. I don't know what it is about books that just feel… homey?"

"I love libraries, my mom is a librarian at a middle school," Valerie smiled. "She raised me with the philosophy that so long as there are libraries, there is hope." Amelia smiled softly as Valerie's cheeks reddened. "Don't mind me, oversharing." Valerie pulled her laptop out of her bag.

"Sustenance," Amelia changed the topic, sliding a bag of trail mix over like an olive branch.

"Oh, yes!" Valerie cheered, "I love the original trail mix."

"That was very enthusiastic," Amelia chuckled.

"It's the only acceptable way to eat raisins," Valerie explained.

"I agree. The chocolate with the fruity sweetness of the raisin and the salty nuts."

Valerie snickered.

"What?" Amelia asked.

"There are so many dick jokes that could follow the phrase 'salty nuts'," Valerie laughed.

"Oh my god," Amelia started laughing too. "Stop distracting me, V."

They each had a laptop open. Valerie got to work editing the footage she had collected to make a trailer for the production. She had spent the late hours of the night after rehearsal watching videos of other *Into the Woods* productions until she stumbled upon a movie version. Valerie had always been able to understand things clearer when given a visual option. Her mother had taught her to compare novels with their film adaptations, but Valerie had always preferred to read the book after watching the movie. When she told Amelia this, Amelia was beyond flabbergasted.

"That's borderline psychotic," Amelia said, her mouth agape.

"That's what my mom says!" Valerie laughed, "But she's the one who ends up disappointed when the movie doesn't match what was in her head."

Now that she had a full idea of the story, she was able to outline some ideas for promotional materials.

Amelia was looking up local listings for any set pieces or costumes that she could buy secondhand for the season. She also edited the rehearsal schedule and put together a program; making sure that she reviewed the cast bios to make sure there were no grammar issues, as well as double and triple checking that everyone's names were correct.

Valerie put the final touches on the trailer and showed it to Amelia. Then they worked together on a posting schedule that would increase in quantity as the show was about to open.

After a few hours of working, both women felt that they had made significant progress on their tasks and that it was time to stop.

"I need to go thrifting," Amelia said. "There are a handful of thrift stores the next town over. I have a lot of props I need to try and find."

"Sure," Valerie said, "I can just head back to my hotel room?" She didn't mean to, but it came out like a question. She didn't want to be alone, and she was really enjoying Amelia's company. "Maybe read a bit before rehearsal or something…"

Amelia laughed, and it was like the chimes of a bell. "You can come with me, you know."

"I didn't want to force you to spend the whole day with me."

"Come on, V, it's always more fun with a friend."

Ah, there it was. Friend. Amelia turned to toss her cup into the recycling and Valerie tried not to let that one word get to her.

Friends was good.

Friends meant they were closer than they had been before.

Friends could be a stepping stone into something more, but it also was a great place to be. *Not that it matters*, Valerie thought. *Just don't be attracted to her; easy.* Valerie looked over at Amelia's long lashes and felt that little flutter. *Or at least don't think about it so much. Yep, easy.*

There was no covert way for her to know if Amelia had any interest in her. It was too soon, which made it too complicated. She was here to do a job and once that job was done, she would be on her way back to Washington. Amelia probably did not want to do a long-distance thing, or maybe she was overwhelmed with the show… or maybe a million reasons. Valerie took a deep breath to slow her racing thoughts and decided to release expectations and just enjoy the day with her new friend.

The pair piled into Amelia's car. "Want the AUX?" she held out the cable to Valerie.

"Sure, what kind of music do you like?"

Amelia started driving and shrugged. "I listen to all kinds of stuff. Broadway, pop, country, some alternative rock style music too."

"Hmm okay let me see." Valerie put one of her playlists on shuffle. The playlist was called *something* and featured some new indie singer/songwriter songs that she had stumbled upon. "I am really into the lyrics of songs. I do not know shit about music composition," Valerie laughed.

Amelia laughed too, "I like the vibe." The soft guitar and melodies flowed through the car. They drove with the windows down along the 78. Now that the marina layer had cleared, the sun was shining. Growing up in Washington, Valerie was used to the overgrowth of green. Trees would create a canopy and the clouds would weigh down from the sky. Washington vegetation was beautiful in the way a weighted blanket was comforting. Southern California was so many different hues. The foothills were covered with trees, but it was more open, and airy.

"There are three different thrift stores I want to go to," Amelia said. "They're all close to each other too so we can just park and walk around."

The first store was called *All Saints* and had little angels on the sign. Cherubs that were dressed to look like Christmas angels with the blue gown and trumpet. Inside was mostly racks of clothes and shelves of glass trinkets. As they combed through each article of clothing, Amelia kept referring to a list on her phone of the actors and their measurements.

"I thought you had a costume designer?" Valerie asked.

"I do, theoretically. She's not super dependable so I just do most of it myself. She helps with alterations though." Amelia said. "Plus, I always like looking through and seeing if I can find anything I want for myself."

They continued through racks of clothes, occasionally picking one up to show the other because of how wild or ridiculous it looked. Eventually, Amelia picked up a sage green blouse that had an old film camera embroidered in brown thread above the heart. "Okay, you need to try this on," Amelia said. "It looks perfect for you." Valerie took it, looked at the tag, and put it back on the rack.

"It's cute, but I'm okay."

Amelia grabbed it again. "At least try it on," she pleaded.

Valerie looked over at the changing area and rubbed her hands on her hips.

"Fine," she said reluctantly, "but you need to try something on too." She handed Amelia a T-shirt with a pig wearing a cowboy on it.

There was only one changing stall if it could be called a stall. It was a corner of the store that had partitions up and a curtain. Amelia went in first. Valerie realized that it was similar to the costume-changing areas Amelia had set up at The Rose.

"Ready or not, here I come!" Amelia cheered as she came out from behind the curtain. She somehow was able to make even the ridiculous shirt look amazing. Amelia had tucked it into the waistband of her light-wash blue jeans. "Howdy, partner. How about you and I go find ourselves some bacon?"

Valerie laughed. "I think you should get it."

"I just might," Amelia stood next to Valerie and turned toward the changing area. "Your turn, V!"

Valerie went in and closed the curtain. She held the shirt in her hands. It was marked as "Large" which sometimes fit her, but sometimes didn't. There was a flare of jealousy at how Amelia was able to fit into damn near anything in this store, and Valerie couldn't.

She took off her tie-dye t-shirt and tossed it onto the stool, the only chair in the small space. Valerie put the blouse on.

"It's... not going to work," she called out.

"Come on, V, let me see it!" Amelia said back, encouragement bright and light in her voice.

Valerie looked in the mirror feeling sick. There was no way she could let Amleia see her in this. The blouse was on, but it was tight. So tight, that Valerie felt like it would tear open if she moved. *This was a mistake,* she thought.

"I'm sure it looks great on you! With the little camera?"

Valerie managed to take off the blouse and quickly put back on her own shirt. She opened the curtain and Amelia's eyebrows came together slightly, a question forming.

"It doesn't fit right," Valerie said.

"We can keep looking," Amelia offered.

"I'd just like to focus on the costumes, if that's okay?" Valerie was confident in herself and her body ninety percent of the time, but that other ten percent was whenever she was shopping for clothes.

Amelia seemed to understand Valerie's shift in demeanor and let it drop. She went back into the changing area to take off the cowboy pig shirt.

"I'm sorry the shirt didn't work out," Amelia said as they started going through racks of clothes again.

"It's fine, clothes shopping and I just don't get along very well. Sometimes, it's like finding a four-leaf clover." Valerie did a double take. "Hey, look at this!" From the rack, she pulled out a shaggy grey faux fur long coat.

"That would be perfect for the Wolf!" Amelia was ecstatic.

She compared the sizing to the actor's measurements. "Look at you, finding four-leaf clovers in a haystack."

Valerie laughed, "Is that how the saying goes?"

"Sure, why not."

The second store was huge. Two stories tall with the narrowest aisles. They combed through the racks of clothes and the shelves of miscellaneous trinkets until they deemed the store was a bust for what they needed. "It was still fun to look around," Amelia said as they went to the final store.

One Man's Treasure had a great haul. Valerie found a wicker basket for Little Red, and two baby dolls. Amelia found a few bundles of fabric, each a different shade of green. "I think it would be really cool to make leaves for the trees out of the fabric. We can make it a cast activity, but it'll make the trees look real. I saw a theatre do this once to make a big willow tree for a production of *A Midsummer Night's Dream*."

"That wasn't on the list though," Valerie noted.

"I know, I was just inspired."

"But you are giving yourself more work to do. I think you should leave the trees how they are."

Amelia bit her lip and looked down at the fabric. "I know it's more work, but it'll really change the whole atmosphere of the set."

"Do you really want to add that much to your to do list? Shouldn't you just stick to the plan? Stay the course?" Valerie asked with genuine concern.

"I…" Amelia struggled to explain. Maybe Valerie was right, maybe it would be too much to take on. But this was part of her vision now. "I want to add it. If I hate it, we'll scrap it, but I want to try it out."

"Okay," Valerie said, "I just don't want you to take on this huge project on top of the other dozens of things I see you already doing. I just see this a lot with clients starting new businesses. They tend to bite off more than they can chew."

Amelia looked insulted. "I know what I can and cannot take on, thank you very much. This is just how I work. Theatre is basically an organic conglomerate. It builds and grows and molds itself into new things by taking parts that belong to something else."

"I just never have done things that way. I mean, in a photo shoot I might try new things and add some props, but most of it I planned out ahead of time. And I will already have an idea of how I want to edit the photos as I take them."

"But do not you let yourself play around and find what works through experimentation?"

Valerie thought for a moment. "Sometimes, but not when I am on a time crunch."

Amelia huffed. "You're not the director, Valerie. I am."

"You're right," Valerie said, "I overstepped. I'm sorry."

There was a glass jewelry case which acted as the check-out counter. Atop it was the cash register, a snake plant in a terracotta pot, and a small dish with spare change in it. The glass case displayed necklaces, earrings, rosaries, rings, and a few dozen enamel pins.

"Oh, I love these!" Amelia said.

"I noticed," Valerie said, gesturing to Amelia's bag that was studded with various enamel pins. One was of Saturn, one of a crystal ball that said, "Future is Female", and about five others.

Amelia pointed out a few pins that captured her interest: a rose, a deck of cards "I love *Alice in Wonderland*", and a succulent.

"I love this one, I think I'd wear it on opening night," she said, holding up a golden rose pin that was about an inch and a half long. "It's more of a broach, so it doesn't quite go with my collection of enamel pins, but it's tradition that actors get flowers at shows. I can get myself this flower." She smiled. "I know it's basic, but roses are my favorite flower. Red roses. They're just timeless and dramatic. And they always make me think of *Phantom of the Opera* and *Beauty and the Beast*."

"So what you are telling me is that you are really into disfigured Frenchmen?" Valerie laughed, taking the gilded rose and looking it over.

Amelia laughed too. "I did not say anything about *Hunchback of Notre Dame*."

"Ah yes, the holy trinity of disfigured French men." Valerie joked and her heart thudded when Amelia threw her head back laughing. "I think it's perfect," Valerie said, handing it back to her.

While Amelia checked out, Valerie noticed that there was one enamel pin, mostly hidden, of a comedy and tragedy mask. It was made of acrylic and covered in glitter. The comedy mask was a shimmering pink, the tragedy mask was seafoam green. Valerie waited until Amelia was leaving to say, "Go ahead and start the car, I need to use the restroom before we head back." As soon as she was outside, Valerie bought the little drama pin and hid it in her laptop sleeve. She wasn't sure why she bought it; an opening night gift, an apology for overstepping, gratitude for their budding friendship? Valerie was a gift-giver. She wanted to get Amelia something, and she decided to hold onto it. The opportunity to gift it would arrive, she was sure.

Chapter 8

On the drive back, Valerie gave the AUX back to Amelia. She played a playlist called "dressing room". "It's just songs from different shows that make me feel pumped up and excited," she explained.

Valerie did not know any of the songs. She enjoyed listening to Amelia sing them out, though. How could one person sound so lovely? How was it that even with the windows down and the music blasting, could Valerie still make out each note sung in Amelia's voice? With each song that came on, Amelia would say, "Oh this is such a good one" or "Listen to this part."

"What is this one about?" Valerie asked sporadically. Amelia would very animatedly explain the characters and why they were singing these songs. "I really do not know a lot of musicals." Valerie admitted.

The shock on Amelia's face was comical. "Are you for real right now? We need to do an emergency education. There are so many!" Valerie laughed at how Amelia's reaction was to launch a crusade against her Broadway ignorance. "Okay, well we have some time before rehearsal. We are going to start you off easy with some movie adaptations. We can watch one before rehearsal?"

"Uh, sure." Valerie hoped she had remembered to leave the marker for housekeeping to come in and make the bed. She had left in a hurry this morning. Amelia started listing a few options, giving short synopses for each. She would not answer any of Valerie's follow up questions to these brief descriptions.

"Spoilers!" Amelia would cry out. "There is just so much I do not want to give away."

They parked in the parking structure next to the hotel. "These things stress me out to drive in," Amelia said, locking the car. "I know my car is short, and there are so many big trucks and stuff that come in here, but I am always stressed that I'm going to hit my roof."

"That's valid," Valerie laughed, "it's almost better to follow someone else in so you can tell that your car is smaller than the one in front of you."

"Yeah!" Amelia said, a little too loudly. Her voice echoed back to them in the concerte structure. Amelia sang a refrain from one of the songs they had just listened to. Valerie was in awe. Her voice was like an orchestra, and she was so bold to sing with abandon even though people would definitely hear her. Valerie wondered what it would be like to have that kind of comfort in your own voice and abilities. Amelia was a wonder, and Valerie was in awe. She shook herself out of it before she started drooling.

"It's so fun to sing in these," Amelia said, oblivious to the fact that Valerie was all but basking in her light. "It would be awful for performances though."

"Yeah, uh, maybe," Valerie was all but incoherent. "Ready?"

Amelia had to try harder than she expected to ignore the fact that Valerie was leading her to a hotel room. It was not a hook up. This was not a hook up. This was... a theatre intervention. *Who hasn't seen Hairspray?* Of course, when they hatched this idea not even thirty minutes ago, she knew that they were going to a hotel. The hotel itself was not a surprise. The surprise was how much nervous energy of anticipation she was feeling.

Nothing is going to happen, Amelia thought. *Just because you are attracted to her doesn't mean she's attracted to you.*

Even so, her heart kicked around inside her ribcage like a horse bucking off its rider when Valerie used her key card to swipe the door unlocked. Thankfully, Valerie could not feel her heartbeat as she opened the door.

A standard hotel room, with a bed, two nightstands, a small desk and once chair. Which meant one of them would need to sit on the bed. *That's fine*, Amelia thought. *Should I? Would it be rude to make her sit in the chair? Would she be more comfortable on the bed? What do I do?*

Valerie seemed to be wondering the same thing. Her eyes were going back and forth from the chair to the bed, sizing her options.

"The chair is not comfortable," Valerie eventually said. Then she went over and sat in the chair.

Amelia shook her head. "No, you need to be comfortable for your musical viewing educational experience. Besides, I would feel bad the whole time. If you are uncomfortable, I will be uncomfortable."

Valerie hesitated, "If you insist."

They each sat on either side of the bed and adjusted the pillows to be back rests. Amelia kicked her shoes off. *You do not put shoes on someone's bed, that's just good manners.*

Valerie crossed her legs on the bed.

They watched the musical on the television. Once the first movie started, Amelia sang along with the opening number, automatically more comfortable.

"Sorry, if I am annoying tell me and I will do my best to stop." She was blushing. Valerie could not stop looking at the peach coloring of her cheeks turn more and more red.

"It's alright," Valerie assured her, "It's like getting two shows at the same time. It makes it more fun to see you enjoy it so much."

Amelia watched Valerie more than she watched the movie. She was still sitting cross legged, leaning back against the pillows, hands folded in her lap. She hadn't adjusted her body language once.

She wondered if she was making Valerie uncomfortable.

As the movie ended, Valerie stretched and stood up. "That was cool. I would love to watch more of these."

"There are some that you can just listen to the soundtrack and it's the whole show."

"They have the spoken parts on the soundtrack too?" Valerie asked.

"No, like, some shows are just singing so the whole show is on the soundtrack."

"Like *Into the Woods*," Valerie said.

Amelia nodded excitedly. "Girl, you have no idea. Some are even more intense than that."

"So, do you prefer musicals?"

"Hmm. I like them a lot. They're fun to watch and fun to be in. Directing them is more work than straight plays."

"Straight plays? As opposed to… gay plays?"

"That's just what non-musical plays are called," Amelia giggled. "Although I guess musicals are pretty gay… in the best way. But to answer your question, no. I prefer theatre that means something. Sometimes that's a musical, sometimes it's a straight play. Theatre that moves people is the theatre I like."

"So, you aren't just doing musical theatre? I don't know any of the other shows on your season list, so I wasn't sure."

"No, I am going to be doing a blend of musicals, new plays, antiquity, and theatre for young audiences. I just wanted to start with a musical to get a strong beginning to the season and the business."

"That makes sense." Valerie nodded. She had to admit that so far, watching musicals had been entertaining, and it was important that The Rose put it's best foot forward and try to entice audiences to return to see plays that they may not have heard of. "Do you think most of your audience will be well versed in the theatre world?"

Amelia shrugged. "Some will be. Some people in the community may come out to see their fellow actor friends, some may just like *Into the Woods*, and I am hoping to get a few tourists as well. It's good that we are so close to the beach because our marquee can attract more people who are here on vacation."

"The location is convenient– it makes marketing for foot traffic really easy."

"Just wait until you see it when it is all lit up," Amelia beamed, although Valerie doubted that any marquee would compare to the sparkle in Amelia's eyes.

Chapter 9

Jason let Valerie in the next day, swinging the door wide, he was wearing deep blue coveralls and worker boots. "Thanks for coming," he said. "I know this is outside of the marketing campaign, but we really appreciate the help."

"Of course," Valerie said. When she had received a call from Jason less than an hour ago, she hadn't known what to expect. He had called the concierge because he didn't know her room number nor have her cell phone. "You said you and Ames needed help?"

"Yes ma'am," Jason led her up the left ramp towards the stage. "I love Amelia, and she's a genius, but I don't have time to help her with the tree thing right now. I need to finish hanging these lights today because the lighting designer is coming tomorrow."

They came around and she saw Amelia sitting on the floor center stage, surrounded by the familiar fabric from the thrift shop. As Valerie got closer, she saw that Amelia was cutting out leaves slightly smaller than the palm of her hand and pinning two together with sewing pins.

"Hey, Ames."

Amelia looked up surprised, "Oh, I didn't notice you come in."

"There's got to be a hundred sets of leaves here."

"Yeah," Amelia gestured to the yards of fabric around her, "with plenty more to go. Do you want to cut or sew? I want to have two pieces of fabric sewn together to make each leaf; it'll give a great flutter effect."

Valerie did her best to hide her reaction. "I can cut, I don't know how to sew."

52

They started to get to work, Valerie cutting along, Amelia sewing, Jason hanging lights with the help of Austin, Paige, and Adam. Once the lights were done, Paige and Adam set up mic packs. Jason and Austin had disappeared to get supplies for the concessions stand.

"Do you think you're doing too much?" Valerie asked, checking in on Amelia. "I mean, can you even accomplish this? It's a lot, plus all the other stuff you do."

"Don't tell me what I can and can't do!" Amelia cried out in frustration. Stark silence. Valerie felt slapped in the face, her chest squeezed.

"Okay," Valerie whispered.

Amelia took a deep breath in through her nose. "I'm sorry, that was too strong," she paused. "My ex-girlfriend was really controlling and micro-managed everything I did. That relationship lasted a year, and I could barely recognize myself by the end of it. One of the first challenges I had to overcome while getting back to myself was replacing the self-doubt with knowing my own limits. I know what I am doing, and I am going to do it."

Valerie nodded. "That makes sense. Obviously, you know your craft better than I do. I just really was looking out for you."

"I know."

Jason came back, followed by Austin and Emily, who plays Baker's Wife. Austin's arm was around Emily's shoulders, and Jason was carrying a bag of some sandwiches.

"Food time, y'all!" Jason called out.

They gathered in the orchestra pit area to eat.

"Thank you all for your help," Amelia said, as everyone was finishing up eating. A chorus of "of course" and "no problems" replied.

"I've got to head out. The wife has stomach aches," Adam said.

"Oh, is she alright?" Jason asked, speaking up for the first time since returning with the sandwiches.

"She's fine, but I told her I'd be home soon."

"Alright, we'll see you later," Amelia said. "Tell Ariel to rest up."

"That's so sweet how he takes care of her," Emily said, looking at Austin.

"Yeah," he agreed. Amelia noticed that Jason wasn't looking, focusing his attention on putting away his trash.

Amelia wanted to redirect the conversation to spare Jason from listening to the showmance between Austin and Emily. "So, V," she said, "what are your life goals?"

Valerie's eyes widened slightly in surprise. Amelia tried to convey the message to please take control of the conversation. Somehow, Valerie picked up on it.

"I want to be a photographer," she said.

"I thought you were? Isn't that why you've been taking all those pictures?" Austin asked.

"No, I work for a social media marketing company, for like, outsourcing your marketing. I think marketing is cool, but I would really like to be a photographer for more than just marketing. Family photos, portraits, photo shoots…" Valerie shrugged.

"So why don't you?" Jason asked.

"I have a lot on my plate with work as it is. Trying to schedule photoshoots in Seattle outside of office hours is hard, and I'm normally so drained at the end of the day; I don't know if it'll ever happen. I just try to get through each day, and Jorge has been overanalyzing everything I do here, and he picks it all apart – even the work I'm proud of," Valerie shook her head. "He puts me through the wringer and then approves it all anyway. It's frustrating. As if I don't normally fix all his stuff for him at work."

"He sounds like an ass," Jason said. Austin, Emily, Paige, and Amelia nodded.

"I'm glad you're here instead," Amelia said, reaching over and holding Valerie's hand, giving it a squeeze.

"Yeah, me too," Valerie said, squeezing back.

"You should try and get some of your own photography stuff while you're here. There are always tons of people taking pictures on the beach," Austin suggested.

Paige started talking about the photographer from her and her husband's wedding. "The photos were good, but she put this filter on them I absolutely hate and I can't take them off and I wish she had just left it how it was!"

Amelia leaned into Valerie's ear and whispered, "If it's something you really want to do, then you'll make it happen."

"Thanks, Ames."

Chapter 10

When Valerie arrived at the theatre before rehearsal the following week, there was an older man talking with Amelia. She had her arms crossed and a defiant look on her face. The man was in his mid-60's and wore a button up collared shirt with a tie. He was blonde but balding, and wore what Valerie assumed were Italian loafers – at least that's what they looked like.

She did not want to seem like she was eavesdropping – although she was – so she walked past the pair with a nod to Amelia, as if to ask *Are you okay?*

Amelia gave a curt nod in response, *Yeah, just annoyed.* That would have been enough, except when Amelia looked back, her eyes narrowed into slits. Suddenly, Valerie felt the chill of a cold shoulder.

"I am a self-made man, Amelia, do you know what that means?" The man said, "I know what it takes to be successful as a business and I am just trying to help you."

Valerie walked past them without breaking stride, with nowhere else to go, she went into the booth, where Jason was adjusting the music cues.

"Who's that?" Valerie asked, gesturing down to where the man was still talking to Amelia, but now was waving his arms around in small circles.

"Amelia's Uncle Glen," Jason replied. "He showed up without warning."

Valerie felt her face turn into a deer-in-the-headlights. "Oh, that's Glen Packet?"

Jason sat up and looked at her, really looked at her. "You talked to him?"

"Uh, he's kind of the one who hired SPRUCE, but I only know his name and relation to Amelia. I've never talked to him before."

Jason nodded with recognition, "That's right, I forgot."

Back in the audience, Glen leaned back in a seat at the front row. Amelia was worried, and Valerie could see the tension in her neck and shoulders. She tried to take a deep breath, but it ended up being too forced and rushed that felt very artificial and not at all helpful.

"Alright everyone, let's run 'The Witch's Rap' from the Prologue and workshop it. Everyone else, you can sit out here and quietly watch, or run lines in the dance room," Amelia said. Some actors sat down, others shuffled to the dance hall through the stage left wings. "Don't drag your feet!" Amelia called out. Once the migrating cast was far enough backstage, Jason pressed play on the little boombox on the edge of the stage.

Amelia was excited to see this number, especially to showcase it in front of her uncle. Ariel, who was playing the witch, was an absolute powerhouse each rehearsal. It was amazing to watch her leave it all on the floor.

"In the past," The Witch began.

And then, instead of doing the blocking they rehearsed last week, she put a hand over her mouth and turned to run off stage. Her husband, Nate, who played the baker was there in a flash with Jack's prop milking pail.

The music continued as Ariel emptied her stomach into the bucket.

Jason stopped the music. "Oh my god," Valerie said, thankful that she hadn't been recording.

Amelia rushed on stage. "Is she okay?"

"Just a stomach bug," Ariel replied. "I think I need to lie down; sorry."

"Don't even worry about it. You guys go home and, please Ariel, rest. Hopefully you feel better tomorrow." Amelia said. She looked over and saw Valerie's concern and her uncle's disappointment all at once.

"Everyone take ten; I'll be right back!" she called out and fled in the direction of her office.

Valerie saw Glen shake his head in disapproval. She followed Amelia out.

"What's going on, Ames?" Valerie asked.

"Seriously?" Amelia was pacing. "You're going to act like you don't know?"

Valerie took a step back with her hands up, "Woah, what did I do?"

"You invited my Uncle Glen to rehearsal!" Amelia burst out. Her face was turning red, her voice betrayed her, expressing that she was on the verge of tears. Valerie shook her head.

"Why would I do that?" she asked. "I have never even spoken with your uncle. I know that he's the one who hired my company, but that's only because it is his signature on the retainer agreement."

Amelia crossed her arms. "Aren't you the one working on my theatre? Or did you lie about that too?"

"I haven't lied, Amelia!"

"You told me that you were personally going to handle the marketing for *Into the Woods* and that you would work with me directly." Her voice growing steady and sharp like a blade for battle. "Now you are trying to undermine me by going to my uncle. He comes in here like I need to be more cooperative. This is *my* theatre, not his." Amelia was looking at her like she was a threat, a snake in the grass.

"Ames," Valerie said, trying to grab her hand, but Amelia pulled it away. "Let me call the office and figure out what is going on. But I promise you, I would never just call your uncle on you. I did not invite him."

"Then who did?"

When Valerie couldn't answer, Amelia crossed her arms and turned away, looking at some paperwork on her desk. Valerie knew she would not get a response just yet, so she went

58

outside to make a call to Matt or Jorge. *Maybe one of them invited Glen down here? Did I miss an email?* Her mind was whirring to try and find the explanation.

She pushed the door to go outside and saw Glen himself on the phone. "Things are not going smoothly here, Luke," he said into his phone. "Your sister is stubborn as usual, and I think the employee that the marketing company sent out is a joke. I asked my niece about it, and she could not get out a coherent sentence about what this Valerie girl had planned."

Valerie cleared her throat as an *I am right here* announcement.

"Ah, here she is. Yes, I will speak with her now. You call the company and demand an update." A pause as Glen and Valerie looked at each other while he listened to the other line. "I don't care that I'm not the business owner, it's my money going into this, paying your paycheck. Figure it out." He tapped the button to end the call with an unnecessary amount of aggression. Valerie put on her customer service smile.

"Hello, I am Valerie." She held out her hand for his to shake. Valerie knew it might be pretentious of her, but she judged people on their handshakes. He shook her hand. She tried to give the right amount of force in the squeeze of her hand-enough to show that she meant business but not so much that the handshake turned into a dick measuring contest. Although she felt like she would win that too.

Glen's handshake was haphazard, lazy, and pompous. He turned his hand in a way that made it seem like Valerie was supposed to kiss his knuckles. And his hand was clammy.

"Green hair is unprofessional," he said.

Valerie was taken aback by his quick cut to personal attacks. "Well, first of all, hello. My name is Valerie. I am going to be handling the marketing for this production as well as building a comprehensive social media presence for…"

"Social media?" Glen cut her off. "I hired your company for a business plan, not to screw around on your phone like a fucking teenager." He looked her up and down with blatant displeasure. "What happened to Jorge?" but he pronounced it 'George' "He was supposed to come down and handle all this."

Ah, the bitter stink of misogyny, Valerie thought. "Sir, social media is the most effective way to promote a business now. Most small business owners must work twice as hard by adding 'content creator' to the many hats they wear. Now, Amelia has a great vision for this play- for this entire theatre. And I am working closely with her and her vision."

Glen huffed and puffed. Valerie had enough experience with entitled clients, that she knew he would cave before blowing the house down.

"Amelia needs to get her head out of the clouds and get a real job. She had one you know. She threw it all away to live in this fantasy land," his eyes scanned the theatre with a sneer. "I told her brother that we should not be enabling her, that I would help her start up a good career in my business. But my nephew insisted that it would be better to be supportive; that she would come to her senses on her own. And I hired you to do that. But when this crashes and burns, you need to have taught her something worth the money I am paying so she can get her life back on track."

Valerie's eyebrows knitted together in frustration and confusion. "Sir, my job is to make sure that Amelia has a comprehensive marketing strategy and a strong start to her season."

Glen crossed his arms. "I want to be clear; Amelia is a smart girl. Do I think she can be successful here?" He shrugged, clearly debating with himself "Sure, maybe. But she could be so much more. White collar professions are generically more reliably successful. All this 'drama' stuff," he used air quotes, "it's a fun hobby. But it shouldn't be her whole life. Women, I mean no offense, you ladies do not have the mental capacity for managing businesses. A business is different than a home."

Oh, you are one of those, Valerie thought, *the misogyny runs deep.*

Valerie tried to control her emotions. She knew he would use that against her, but she hated being berated. She took a stabilizing breath and tried again. "Sir," she started, but he cut her off.

"Now, in my day, we knew that the client is always right. I am the client. You will do what I say, or when this business fails, I will make sure that you will never be hired to use a camera again! You seem smart enough to understand." With that, he stood straighter and put on his sunglasses. "I am a very powerful man, Valerie. And I will not tolerate being dismissed or ignored. I don't just want you to keep the ship from sinking, but if Amelia has any hope for getting this off the idea board and into a reality, then you better convince *me* that this isn't a waste of not only my resources, but of her potential. Luke, he has his own ideas. Perhaps he's a bit misguided by Amelia's enthusiasm, but he wanted to give her a chance. Don't make me regret agreeing to it."

Glen left and Valerie saw an email from Jorge and one from Matt. Jorge's read: "Make sure you keep in contact with Glen and/or Luke. Glen is upset. You need to keep him in the loop. It's unprofessional to dodge a client's calls and emails."

Valerie scrunched her brows. Glen had not reached out to her once this entire time. What was this about? And who did Jorge think he was to tell her to talk to clients when he never answered their calls and usually made assistants answer his emails?

Somehow, Matt's email was worse: "Client on the theatre file is displeased with your performance. If it's too much for you, I will send someone else out there. Jorge is out of quarantine now."

Valerie's heart dropped into her stomach like a stone into a pond. She didn't want to leave. She wanted to help Amelia, she wanted to launch herself out of editorial and into a photographer's position. She typed out a quick email back to both: "Communication error has been corrected. I spoke with the client, and we are on the same page now. I will send a detailed update tomorrow."

Things were going to be a lot more complicated. How was she supposed to prove that she could handle helping businesses succeed to her boss when the client was ordering her to help it fail?

    What the fuck am I going to do?

Chapter 11

Amelia was back to directing by the time Valerie returned inside. Amelia tried not to look at her, but she could tell by the sag in Valerie's shoulders that something was off. Amelia wasn't sure if she was mad or not, but it had felt like a betrayal when she came to The Rose just to be confronted with Uncle Glen. If Valerie really hadn't invited him here, then she felt bad for exploding on her.

Valerie worked silently setting up a backdrop for character photos. A lot of the cast was excitedly talking to her, but Valerie was only mildly interested.

"Great work," Amelia said to the actors on stage. "Go get ready for your character photos."

"You okay?" Jason asked.

"I need to apologize to her, I think."

"What happened?"

Amelia cradled her head in her hands, "I kind of blew up on Valerie and accused her of going behind my back and inviting Uncle Glen here."

Jason's eyes widened, "No, she didn't!"

"How do you know for sure?"

"Because when she got here, she didn't know who he was and told me that she had never talked to him."

Amelia groaned, "Damn. I really messed up. When she's done with the photos, I should talk to her."

"You should definitely do that."

Valerie fell into her element taking promotional photos. The cast was so fun to work with. She did some group photos that ended up being like living murals. Amelia and her had moved into a creative space that left the unresolved conflict at the door. They were collaborating on directing the cast into great moments.

By the end, they had some great options for the program, poster, and social media posts.

"The individual headshots will be posted on the callboard in the lobby during the show so people can see them as they wait for the house to open," Amelia said at the end-of-rehearsal-circle.

"And I will also email them out to each of you so you can use them as a profile photo on your different social media platforms to help promote the show," Valerie added. "You guys were amazing, and we got some really great shots. Give yourselves a hand!" Valerie was so pumped she almost forgotten all about Glen Packet.

When the cast left to change out of their costumes, Valerie went to dismantle her backdrop that she had set up for the character headshots. Amelia followed her timidly.

"Hey," she said lamely.

"Hey, Ames." Valerie kept working.

"Can I help?"

"Sure, can you wrap up the cables for these lights?"

Amelia started looping the cables to put them away. "I need to apologize." Valerie said nothing. Amelia took a deep breath. "I really blew up on you without reason. I should have talked to you, or at least listened to you. When I showed up and Uncle Glen was here, I just assumed…"

"Well, you know what they say about when you assume," Valerie said, placing the folded backdrop into her case, "you make an ass of you and me."

"Mostly me this time," Amelia replied. Valerie nodded in agreement. "I just wanted to say sorry. So, I'm sorry."

Valerie let out a breath. "I forgive you. It was a lot, and after my short conversation with Glen, I can empathize with how you must have been feeling."

"You guys talked?"

Valerie explained how she had caught Glen outside when she went to call her boss. "It was more of a lecture than a conversation, he really likes to hog the speaking time."

Amelia laughed weakly in agreement.

"Anyway, he basically wants me to make sure The Rose is successful as if I am making the whole business plan."

"That's not your job, though," Amelia said, "It's mine."

"I know, but he was really weird about it. He was telling me I had to convince him that the theatre would be successful," Valerie packed the last of her things. "I know you've got this though, Amelia. And I think he does too, he's just worried about you. He shows it like a total ass, but I think it comes from a place of love."

Amelia nodded, "It does. I'm lucky to have someone looking out for me, but sometimes it feels too… restrictive."

"Oh, absolutely. I've only had one conversation with him, and I can tell he's a hard ass." They laughed together and walked through the building, locking up and making sure that the cast had all left.

"I really am sorry, V," Amelia said. "There's really no excuse for me blowing up on you."

"I know you are. Forgiven and forgotten. Trust me, my ex would blow up on me for the most random and irrational things," Valerie tried to laugh it off, but she felt awkward. "Oversharing again, my bad."

"You can tell me, if you want to," Amelia said. They had made their way back into the lobby at this point and were sitting on the floor, watching the cars drive by through the glass doors.

"Stacy and I… we were together for eight months. She… well, she was a real fighter. About anything. Sometimes I felt like she would pick a fight just because she was bored."

"What kind of fights?" Amelia said, unable to hide the worry in her voice.

"Nothing physical, or anything like that. Well, one time she threw a shoe at me." Amelia covered her mouth with a hand. "It missed," Valerie hurried on. "Anyway, she was always thinking I was being too controlling if I tried to plan a date night or something. She also thought I was cheating on her any time it took me longer than an hour to reply to a text. Sometimes I was at work, or asleep! She worked a lot of nights as a bartender, and I typically work an 8 to 5, so she'd text me at two in the morning and would get mad at me for not replying. She'd come home and turn the lights on like she was trying to catch me between the legs of another woman."

"Wow," Amelia said.

"Yeah, sorry. That was probably too descriptive." Valerie ran her hands through her hair starting at the base of her neck and combing up. "Turns out, she was cheating on me. Again. So, I ended it with her and came here."

"Wait, back up. What do you mean again?" Amelia asked.

Valerie explained the circumstances of how their relationship started. "I don't know why I thought it was okay. Either she convinced me or I convinced myself that she had been wronged by her ex and needed an out and somehow that she fell in love with me. Stacy was a lot of things, but she made me feel beautiful." Valerie shook her head, "That's probably not enough to base a relationship on, but for a while we were comfortable together. I don't know." Valerie shifted a little and crossed her legs. "I have always struggled to feel beautiful. It feels like femininity is just barely unattainable."

"V, you *are* beautiful," Amelia said. It pained her to hear Valerie dismiss herself like this.

Valerie waved a dismissive hand, "Yeah, I know. But I mean there's an aspect of feminine beauty and grace that is so associated with being dainty and fragile and soft. And I want to be those things. I want to be the porcelain ballerina doll with the beautiful gowns… but I'm not dainty. I'm not an ingénue. And it's okay. I just mean, she could make me feel like that sometimes. Especially in the beginning. But then I felt like an old toy that lost its appeal."

"You have plenty of appeal, V," Amelia said before she could stop herself.

Valerie looked at her, and Amelia blushed and focused on the hem of her jeans.

They sat in silence for a bit before Amelia asked, "So you guys were serious then? Like thinking about getting married?"

"Ha! Stacy didn't want to get married. She said that it felt too patriarchal. And I always wanted to get married someday, but I just sort of... well, she didn't want to get married so I would say that I didn't care either way."

"But you did care." Amelia said. A statement, not a question.

"Yeah, I want to get married someday. When I find the right person."

"Me too, someday."

They waited in a few moments of comfortable silence, absorbing what they each had said. There was a building of energy between them. Suddenly, a car backfired on a nearby street making both Amelia and Valerie jump.

Chapter 12

As the week went by, Amelia and Valerie had fallen into a groove in rehearsals. Valerie was able to get great testimonials from cast members when they weren't on stage. They'd talk about how the theatre had been a home to them, and about how Amelia was great to work with. Valerie started to think about using the footage as a closing night farewell to her as a director from the cast. She'd have to ask Jason about that.

As if he could hear her thoughts, Jason came around the corner into the dressing room. "Have you seen Amelia?" he asked.

A chorus of no's and shaking heads. Without another word, Jason left.

Valerie followed him out. "What's going on?"

"I think our Jack's mom is dropping the show."

"Wait, can she do that? This close to the show? Opening night is the weekend after next…"

As they came around the skrim wall, they saw Amelia in the booth. Jason called out to her, "Houston, we have a problem."

They went into the tech break room, Amelia shut the door. "What's wrong?"

Jason explained that an actress was dropping the show, and that they needed to find a replacement fast.

"Aren't there… understudies or something?" Valerie asked.

"She was the understudy, she had to jump in early on when the woman we originally cast ended up having to move out of state because her husband's work relocated them," said

Amelia. "The role must be cursed or something." She took a moment. "Does the cast know?"

"Not yet, I don't think. No one has said anything to me."

"Okay, I'll let them know before we start the run tomorrow. Most of them are gone by now anyway. Casting is my responsibility as the director, so I'll just figure this out."

Jason and Valerie shared a look. Already they could see that Amelia's eyes were unfocused as she ran through possible solutions rapidly.

"It is up to you, but you don't have to do it alone," Valerie said. "How can we help?"

"Maybe we can call someone from auditions?" Jason suggested, pulling out some forms from his show binder.

"Maybe." Amelia seemed unsure to go back through the people she had not initially cast.

"Do you remember Claire from callbacks?" Jason suggested. "She was really good."

"She is more than good, she's exceptional," Amelia conceded. Valerie wondered why she felt jealous of some other girl being noted for her talent when Valerie had no desire to have the same talent… Maybe it was just the way Amelia seemed to admire this Claire person. "Which is why she got the part of one of the Leading Player in *Pippin* at Limelight Theatre in Temecula." Amelia sighed. "I could call around some other actors in the community. But if they did not initially audition, it feels weird to ask them to be in the show."

Jason nodded and flipped through some papers.

"What are those?" Valerie asked, gesturing to the papers.

Jason shook their head, "These are just the audition forms. I keep all of them, even the ones Amelia did not cast, just in case."

"Are there any other options?" Valerie asked, trying to get a grasp of the situation.

Amelia ran her fingers through her hair, "Not really. There was another woman who would be a good age for the role,

Pam, but her audition wasn't very strong. And I do not know if I want to risk the energy of the show if that makes sense."

Jason shrugged. "It's community theatre, Amelia. You use what you can get… and sometimes that isn't super great, but it's part of the whole thing. Some of our community is better than others, but some of them just do this for fun."

Amelia laid back and looked up at the lights. "Pam is great. But her memorization isn't all there at her age… I am going to call someone I have in mind first, and then Pam. I just really do not want to throw a wrench in the energy of the cast. We have a really good thing going."

"And if nothing else, maybe you could throw Valerie on stage," Jason quipped.

Valerie let out a nervous laugh, "Please do not, I am not a stage person, I can not even talk on stage, let alone sing."

Jason and Amelia looked at her like they did not believe her.

"I am dead serious," Valerie continued, "I was in orchestra as a kid, but only because cellos are sitting, and I could hide behind my sheet music. And I always let Jessie McFoles be first* cello, so he was blocking me from the audience."

They blinked at her in response, then a second later, all three of them were laughing and holding their sides, bursting at the seams. Amelia was holding her sides and wiping a tear from her eye.

"Yeah, let's not use Valerie as a backup actor," she said. "She'll stay in the booth with me."

With me.

Valerie tried not to analyze the tingling feeling in her chest at those words.

"Well, someone needs to keep you company up there, since I will be on deck." Jason agreed. "On deck means I will be running around like a chicken with his head cut off trying to get everyone in place and fixing costume malfunctions, broken props, or anything that goes wrong. All in the effort to make sure the audience never notices that anything was amiss."

Valerie was amazed. "That's… a lot. Do things normally fall apart like that?"

Amelia shook her head. Jason sipped their coffee before responding, "Not all at once, but something is always going to happen. Better to be prepared and have someone in the wings ready to jump into action."

"And you and I will be on headset," Amelia continued, while she typed away on her phone.

Valerie felt warmth creep up her neck. "Why do I need to be on headset?"

Amelia looked up grinning, "Because our light board operator is going to jump onstage as Jack's mom."

Jason gasped excitedly, "Sarah? Are you for real?" When Amelia nodded, Jason squealed. "She has been off stage for too long."

"Ever since she had her baby a few years ago," Amelia confirmed, "She had stopped performing for a while because being a new mother is hard, breastfeeding, postpartum, you name it. Then when her baby was older and she was ready to perform, she had lost her confidence to audition."

"So how do you know she'll do it?" Jason asked.

Amelia held up her phone. "I sent her a text. Isn't modern technology just the best?"

Valerie smiled, "Well, I am glad you are providing the opportunity for her." Then an idea hit her, "I have been gathering little testimonials from different cast members about what they love about this theatre and why they chose to be a part of this production."

"Oh, that's what you've been doing, this whole time I thought you were just Amelia's eye candy" Jason teased as they downed the rest of their coffee, "I want to do one."

Amelia looked like a deer in the headlights, and Valerie felt herself blush.

"Bye, Ms. Director Lady. I have an exclusive interview and I don't need you hovering while I give my hot takes." Jason shooed Amelia away with the back of his hand. "My paparazzi awaits!" Amelia threw her hands up in mock defeat and left for the office.

Valerie set up her portable tripod and camera. "Let's get started. First question, what can you tell me about why you are working here at the theatre?"

"Amelia is my best friend, and she is so dedicated to her art. When she told me she was opening her own theatre, I knew I wanted to come work for her. It's hard to find an employer who cares as much as she does, or a workplace that really feels like a family."

Valerie smiled; she had felt that same energy from Amelia since their first meeting in the office.

"Next question," she continued, "give me a pitch for *Into the Woods*, why should people come see it?"

Jason thought about this one a bit longer. "It's a great story, blending so many of our most beloved fairy tales. It has something for everyone."

"Very diplomatic," Valerie noted.

"I think you mean capitalist," Jason countered.

"Close enough," Valerie laughed. "Okay final question: What is your favorite part of the show?"

"Agony, hands down." Jason said without hesitation.

"Can you explain for the camera?" Valerie asked.

"Oh right, there's a song called *Agony* between the two brothers, Cinderella's Prince and Rapunzel's Prince. It's a hilarious scene and I already know it's going to be a crowd favorite. Besides, Austin is just really talented."

"Oh yeah?" Valerie asked.

Jason blushed slightly. "You've seen him; don't you think he's great?"

Valerie had to agree, and she felt herself smile. It was obvious to her that there was something going on beneath the surface. She closed her camera. "Alright," she said, "I think that's great. I can build off each of those questions and ask people throughout the next two weeks their responses too, and then I can compile them."

Jason jumped up, "Sweet."

"Can I ask you something?" Jason nodded and Valerie continued. "Are you crushing on Austin?"

Jason blanched and blanched at the same time, and Valerie wondered if she stumbled on something too sensitive.

"Are you crushing on Amelia?" he asked back.

"Touché."

Jason shook his head and stared at his shoes. "Austin and I have a history."

"I thought he was with the Baker's Wife, what's her name? Emily?"

"If they're anything it's a showmance." At Valerie's confused face, he continued. "A fling that happens between cast members during a show. Normally their characters have some kind of intimacy but not always."

"Huh, that's interesting."

"So, you and Amelia? Is that a showmance or is it something more?" Jason asked, changing the subject.

"I don't know. It's probably… something," she said lamely.

They let the conversation drop as understanding settled between them.

"Amelia cannot know," Jason said. "There's… history. And I can't… It's just… I love her, but I'd rather keep it to myself for now."

"I get that," Valerie said. "She has a lot on her plate. I don't want to overwhelm her either." She hoped he understood her meaning. He gave her a sad look.

"I think you'd be good for her." Jason said. "Not that this conversation ever happened, but one of you needs to make the first move. I will stay out of it."

Chapter 13

After Jason's interview, the trio decided to grab some Korean BBQ. "Twenty-five dollars per person, but all you can eat for an hour and a half." Jason said.

"Is it healthy? It probably could be," Amelia said, "but not the way we do it."

"Beef and rice, bay-bee!" Jason chanted as they walked in the door.

Each table had a small grill in the center of it, and there was a salad bar as well with a rice cooker at one end.

"Get the salt," Amelia said.

"Way ahead of you," Jason replied.

They were seated at a booth towards the front. Amelia and Valerie sat in the chairs on one side, Jason sat on the booth on the other side with their purses.

Jason ordered a Dr. Pepper, Amelia a Cherry Coke, and Valerie a Sprite.

"I am a clear soda elitist," Valerie said when their drinks arrived.

"Wait, Pepsi or Coke?" Amelia asked.

"Umm, Coca-Cola has Sprite, so Coke?"

"Ha!" Amelia cried triumphantly in Jason's face. "Coke is better than Pepsi, it is the ultimate American soda."

Jason rolled his eyes as the waiter brought them a plate of raw beef slices that looked curled. Valerie was a bit concerned by the raw meat.

"You cannot even count her vote, 'clear soda elitist' my ass," Jason said.

"Wow, suddenly drinking Sprite made me a second-class citizen," Valerie joked. She watched Amelia take some tongs and started to cook the beef.

Jason handed each of them a small bowl of rice. He also had a saltshaker and an empty plate.

"So, how does this work?" Valerie asked.

Amelia and Jason stared at her. "Hold on, have you never had Korean BBQ before?" Valerie shook her head no slowly. "Oh my god," Jason said, "Give her the first piece!"

"Salt!" Amelia said.

Valerie's teeth were clenched, her hands clammy. This was a lot of attention at once., even though it was just two people. *Having people watch you eat is so freaking uncomfortable,* Valerie thought.

Amelia put a piece of beef brisket on her little bowl of rice with a pinch of salt. They were both watching her intently, silently. The pop music playing, the sizzling of the beef still cooking, the chatter of the wait staff in the back of the restaurant.

"You guys are making me nervous," Valerie said.

"Eat it!" They cried back.

Valerie had never been so self-conscious to eat a singular bite of food before. It felt excruciatingly drawn out. *How do you make eating with chopsticks not awkward when the girl you like is sitting next to you?* She wished she could fall out of the chair, that would be less stressful. When she finally tasted the salty beef and sticky white rice, Jason and Amelia cheered.

"It's pretty good," Valerie said.

"Yep!" Amelia agreed, helping herself to some of the beef straight from the grill into her rice bowl.

"Technically, you can add more flavors or different meats, but we are boring and basic." Jason said.

"And we like it that way." Amelia added. They clinked their cups together.

"Are you going to come to the skate rink?" Jason asked.

"Umm, when?"

"It's a cast bonding thing we are going to do closer to tech week," Amelia explained.

"That sounds fun," Valerie said.

About twenty minutes had passed by when Jason checked his phone. "I actually have to go, I have a meeting in town," he said.

"Meeting? For what?" Amelia asked.

"Just a person coming to the house to measure the walls. Aunt Kennedy is thinking of remodeling. But since she's off on her adventure in Denmark, I need to let the measuring people in," Jason took another swig from his drink and tossed two twenties on the table. "Bye bye," he said. Valerie could've sworn he had tried to wink at her as he left.

"And then there were two," Amelia said. Since Jason had left, they each decided to break up the beef and rice with a salad. Hers had mandarin oranges, chickpeas, and sesame seeds with a light poppyseed dressing.

Valerie's had corn, peas, lima beans, carrot strips, croutons and thousand island dressing. "A pair of salad eating heathens," Valerie joked. "What would dear Jason say?"

Amelia laughed, "Probably something just like that." She considered what she should say next as she watched Valerie stack the empty plates on the edge of the table. "Have you worked in food before?"

"No, but my mom did before she became a librarian. It's just how she raised me; it's a habit now to stack things up," Valerie said.

"And your dad?"

Valerie fell silent. Immediately, Amelia knew she had taken the wrong path, placed her foot on the wrong steppingstone. Valerie deflated; her eyes dropped to her plate.

"I'm sorry, you don't have to," Amelia apologized but Valerie shook her head.

"No, it's okay, my dad was in a plane crash. No survivors…" Valerie trailed off.

"I am sorry." Amelia said, because what else was there to say?

"I was really little. I don't really remember him, but my mom tells me about him all the time."

"That's sweet."

"Yeah," Valerie smiled softly down at her plate. "You're close to your mom then?"

Valerie looked up. "She's my best friend."

There we go, back on solid ground, Amelia thought.

"What about your parents?" Valerie asked.

Never mind. "My dad was in business with Uncle Glen, my mom's brother. Then Mom and Dad got married, had their two kids, decided that maybe they shouldn't have done that. They got divorced when I was thirteen. So, you know, super fun."

"Oh, Amelia, I didn't-" Valerie started.

"Please, don't worry about it," Amelia said. "Shit happens. Honestly, I am lucky that my parents were able to co-parent. I mean, it can't be easy to see your ex every day. They put my brother and I first, and that really meant everything." She took a deep breath. Valerie waited for her to continue, and she wondered briefly how long Valerie would let the silence linger. "It all went to shit after I came out though. My dad was adamant that I was a lesbian out of rebellion in the wake of the divorce. He came around, but it was nasty for a while. Brutal. He took it out on my mom and then she took it out on him… it was a whole ordeal. We had counseling and once Luke and I aged out of the family court jurisdiction, my parents did not need to deal with each other on a regular basis."

"Where are they now?"

"Dad moved to Japan to teach on the military base to the kids, and Mom works at a car dealership in Idaho."

"Idaho?"

"Yeah, she says she loves it there. She hadn't really been interested in being a mom, I think. She has her own life now and that's that. My dad and I don't really talk since I came out. Sometimes he reaches out, but I don't know what kind of relationship I want with him, if that makes sense." After a moment, "Anyway, I should probably start to head home. I have some stuff to take care of."

"For sure," Valerie said. "I wish we could hang out all night. This was fun."

"Yeah, almost like a date," Amelia said.

"Almost." Valerie agreed.

"Except," Amelia said leaning forward, "when we do go on a date, we won't have Jason as a third wheel for half of it." She reached across the table and interlocked her fingers with Valerie's, "I'll hold your hand, and I might even kiss you before we sit down to eat."

Valerie felt her face warm. "Too bad this isn't a date," she said quietly.

Amelia stood up and whispered in her ear, "Maybe next time." Then she walked away to pay the bill.

Valerie composed herself and followed her outside.

"We should plan a movie night," Amelia said casually. "Like a movie marathon. You have more musicals to watch."

"Yeah, that'd be nice," Valerie said.

"How about the week after opening?"

"I have a TV we can use."

"And room service!" Amelia smiled.

They stood there for a moment, just smiling stupidly at each other. Valerie wanted to kiss her, to hold her.

"Have a good weekend, V," Amelia purred.

"See you Monday, Ames."

Chapter 14

Amelia was in the middle of folding laundry when Jason arrived. He let himself into the apartment as he usually did.

"I have some steaming fucking hot tea and it needs to be served. The laundry can wait." He sat on the couch, but he was restless. His legs were bouncing, and he kept rubbing his hands together.

"What's going on?" Amelia asked.

"You know how Aunt Kennedy had remodeling people come over yesterday?" Amelia nodded. "Well, they weren't just remodeling people, it was a moving company. They showed up with boxes and luggage and at first, I thought Aunt Kennedy must have had a big spending spree and I even joked about it with one of the workers. Except the joke fell flat and it was awkward because he was just like 'I just work here'. Anyway, then I noticed a bag that had a name tag on it, but it did not say Kennedy Payne, it said Rhett Jennings!"

"Who's that?" Amelia asked.

Jason lifted his hands over his head. "Thank you! Exactly! That's what I wanted to know. So, I called Aunt Kennedy, and get this." He leaned in conspiratorially, "She eloped."

"What?" Amelia's jaw dropped.

"I know!"

"Who is he?"

"I guess he's an old flame or whatever; I did not get a lot of details from the woman. She was all excited and she said she hired a wedding planner and that she's going to have a wedding ceremony here literally tomorrow." He shook his head in disbelief.

"That is… wow… very fast."

"Right? And they say lesbians move fast, but here you and Valerie are moving as swift as molasses."

"First of all, that's a stereotype. And second, I refuse to acknowledge whatever you think you are talking about. And third, we are supposed to be talking about Aunt Kennedy. If you want to talk about our love lives, I am more than willing to hear more about yours."

"What do you mean mine? I am a single pringle."

"Perhaps. I think you are talking to someone because you did not mention once that any of the workers were attractive, and you always think watching men do physical labor is hot."

Jason smiled bashfully. "If I had something to share with the class, I would bring it to show and tell."

"Oh, so there is someone?" Amelia said.

"Back to Aunt Kennedy!" Jason laughed as he changed the subject. "She wants a wedding. And I'm the best man. And you are the maid of honor."

Amelia put her hands to her heart, "Aww, really?"

"Yes. But she literally will not have time for a bachelorette party because she's coming back from Denmark right now and they're landing in LA at like midnight, so she wants to rest before the ceremony tomorrow."

"Midnight tonight?"

Jason nodded.

"This is insane." Amelia shook her head.

"It is, and honestly, I want her to be happy. That's the most important thing. Happy and safe. Fuck, I hope this guy isn't some creepy serial killer or scam artist. I hate that I will not get to meet him until the ceremony."

"Oh, yeah that's a big yikes. What about living there? I assume she'll want to live with her spouse, would you be comfortable with that."

"Ew. Umm, I don't know. I think I might need to move. She mentioned that he travels a lot for work so maybe she'd be with him? I don't know. I am going to feel it out for a while."

"Where did he live before Denmark?"

"Alabama, I think," Jason said with a frown. Southern states were not known for being accepting of transgender or queer people.

"I am sure Aunt Kennedy would not be with someone that wasn't an ally at minimum." Amelia said, sensing his concerns.

"Yeah, that's probably true. It's weird though, right?"

"It's fast." Amelia said.

"Can we change the subject? I'm exhausted from it already." Jason adjusted on the couch. "For example, why don't you want to talk about V?"

"There's nothing really to talk about."

"Yeah, uh, tell that to your face."

Amelia groaned, "I may have told her that I would want to kiss her last night, but she didn't say anything, and I might have laid it on too thick."

"Oh. My. God." Jason started laughing.

"No, seriously, maybe she just thought I was joking? Maybe she's not into me."

"Amelia."

"Jason."

Jason gave her a teasing smile. "Well, maybe she wants to go out with me."

That made Amelia laugh, "Jason, you're gay. And so is she."

"See how ridiculous that sounds? It's almost as ridiculous as you thinking Valerie doesn't like you." Jason got up to leave.

"You think so?" Amelia

Jason shrugged, "You're gonna have to let me know if I'm right."

Chapter 15

Amelia woke up early on Saturday morning. She was determined to wait and see if Valerie would text her first today, especially after confessing to wanting to kiss the other day. Yesterday after Jason left, they texted a bit, but it was mostly work related. Different filter options for photos. Besides, she needed to focus on Aunt Kennedy. Not Valerie, or the way her curves filled out her jeans… nope. Definitely not thinking about Valerie today.

"Good morning, best man," she said when Jason picked up the phone.

"Hrmm." Jason mumbled back.

"It's wedding day, let's get it moving. I'm outside."

Amelia handed him his coffee as he got in the car. "It's too early."

"Yep, but we need to get the ceremony ready for Aunt Kennedy."

"I cannot believe she's getting married." Jason said. "I thought she was going to be a single wine aunt forever."

"It's happening fast too. She just met this guy in Denmark last week?" Amelia asked.

"No, they knew each other. They just reconnected last week," Jason corrected, taking a sip of coffee. "Shit, it's hot!"

"I would've gotten iced coffee but I know you hate when it gets watered down, and you take forever to get up."

Jason shrugged.

They pulled up to the wedding venue. It was an outdoor property, with some water scaping. There were white folding chairs set up. At the front, there was a trellis covered in honeysuckle and ivy. Amelia approached a worker to see if there was anything she could do to help set up.

"No, ma'am we've got it covered." He said with a slight southern drawl.

"Babies!" Aunt Kennedy called out. Amelia and Jason smiled and rushed over to her. "Time to prepare the bride!" They walked over and saw her clad in a pink silk robe that sprawled along the floor after her, every bit as dramatic and regal as a golden age movie star. Aunt Kennedy was a gorgeous black woman in her fifties. She had on a short black wig that was styled with cascading waves. She was steady, and so unabashedly herself that she felt like home and maternal love to Amelia for as long as she had known her.

They went into a small white and blue farmhouse. Aunt Kennedy had dropped everything off the night before. Her beautiful wedding dress was hung on the wall with Amelia's dress and Jason's suit on either side. The dress was floor-length with a small train. It had iridescent beading along the structured lace bodice and flowed down in an A-shape. It had a swooping neckline, and the balloon sleeves were sheer under the lace.

"It means so much to me that both of you are here," Aunt Kennedy's warm voice chimed from behind them.

"You look amazing!" Jason said, twirling her around.

"Traveling keeps me young, and engagement adds its own glow," Aunt Kennedy beamed, showing off the ring on her finger. It was silver with a topaz in the center surrounded with a dozen tiny diamonds.

"Tell us about him!" Amelia smiled. She did not want to come off as apprehensive, but she was curious.

The smile on Aunt Kennedy's face only widened. "Oh, he's wonderful; his name is Rhett. We knew each other lifetimes ago doing our undergraduate work in Alabama."

"That is so sweet," Amelia swooned.

"Where has he been this whole time? What happened?" Jason asked.

"Well, I moved back to California, and he stayed in Alabama for a while until his career in architecture took off. Now he's a consultant for a huge company and they were opening a new branch in Denmark. We ran into each other one morning in line for coffee. We talked briefly but he had a meeting to get to. And then we saw each other in the same spot every day until he finally asked me to join him for dinner. It was like no time had passed."

"Excuse me, ma'am?" A young woman with slick black hair wearing a pantsuit came into the room. She folded her hands apologetically. "We just received word that your photographer had a family emergency and cannot make it to the ceremony. Do you have someone else in mind?"

Aunt Kennedy looked stricken. "No photographer? But I want to commemorate today," she looked at Amelia and Jason. "Could one of you...? I mean, that's not ideal; I do want all of us in the pictures together..."

"I know someone!" Amelia said, quick to problem solve. *Just problem solving,* she thought, *This is to help Aunt Kennedy, it's not like it's for me.*

Jason looked at her knowingly, and the pantsuit lady grabbed everyone a glass of champagne.

"Call them, then!" Aunt Kennedy cheered.

Amelia walked over to the archway connecting the kitchen and living room area and hovered over Valerie's contact information in her phone. She hesitated for a moment, wondering if this was going to come off as desperate.

"Tell them I will pay double!" Aunt Kennedy laughed. Amelia hit the call button and put the phone up to her ear, and attempted to lean against the wall. But there was so much energy in her now, like a buzzing. Part of her wanted to blame the coffee.

"Hello?" Valerie answered on the second ring.

"Hey, V. It's Amelia, are you busy? Like, for the rest of the day?" Amelia tried (and failed) to keep the buzzing energy out of her voice.

"I'm just reading. Everything okay?" Valerie replied.

Amelia felt the relief wash through her like a cool breeze, and also a sense of joy and excitement. "Get dressed, something business professional and yet comfortable if you have it."

"Not white or black!" Aunt Kennedy cried out.

"Nothing black or white, if possible," Amelia parroted.

"Uh, that's not what... Why?"

She could hear the confusion and hesitation in Valerie's voice. It wasn't until this moment that she realized she hadn't explained anything to Valerie. "I'm at a wedding and I desperately need a photographer." Amelia pleaded. She tried to hide the pleas from the ears in the room. It appeared everyone else was admiring the dress and drinking their champagne. "I know it's last minute, but Aunt Kennedy will compensate you."

Amelia waited while Valerie on the other side of the phone call considered.

Finally, after an eternal moment, Valerie responded. "Can you come pick me up? I had my car taken in for an oil change."

"Yes! Thank you so much! You're a lifesaver. I will be there in fifteen minutes." Amelia hung up the phone and announced that the photographer was secured, and she was going to go pick her up.

"You mean your girlfriend," Jason teased.

Aunt Kennedy turned. Her eyes sparkled like the champagne in her glass.

"Not my girlfriend," Amelia corrected, pained to see the light in Aunt Kennedy's eyes dim even a fraction. "She's just helping with the marketing for the startup of the theatre."

"And you think she's hot," Jason goaded on.

Aunt Kennedy raised her eyebrows.

Amelia felt her defenses rise in response.

"I look forward to meeting her," Aunt Kennedy said. "Girlfriend or not."

Amelia blushed the whole way to pick up Valerie, replaying the word in her head.

Girlfriend.

Valerie was outside wearing a button up short sleeve top that was blush pink on one side and maroon on the other, and grey pants. She paired the outfit with a delicate silver necklace and cream-colored snakeskin boots. Her hair was in space buns which showed off the aquamarine color underneath. Amelia wondered how soft they were.

On the drive back, Valerie was looking through some photography poses and ideas online while Amelia filled her in on the wedding party and described the venue and small size of the bridal party. She wondered to herself if she needed to warn Valerie that Aunt Kennedy was a notorious matchmaker, but decided against it, fully believing that the day would be all consuming and Aunt Kennedy would be focused on her new husband.

When they arrived, Valerie let out a soft "Oh wow." The ceremony area had been finished. On the left was a post clock, white with ribbons and tulle wrapped around it. On the right, a lamp post similarly decorated.

Jason stood in the aisle, "Aunt Kennedy said guests will be arriving soon. She wants some 'getting ready' photos."

"Sounds good!" Amelia led Valerie back to the cottage.

Aunt Kennedy greeted them both with a hug. "I am so glad you are here," she told Valerie.

Amelia got dressed and styled Aunt Kennedy's hair. Valerie took some photos and asked questions about her and the groom. When Amelia went into the kitchen to get another bottle of champagne, she hesitated and listened.

"And what about you, dear?" Aunt Kennedy asked Valerie. "Tell me, do you have a special someone?"

Valerie smiled, "No ma'am, but today is about you."

"I am the bride, and it's bad luck to say no to the bride."

"I think you made that up," Jason said.

"It's not worth the risk! Humor me. Tell me about your love life." Aunt Kennedy took a sip out of her champagne flute.

"I am not currently in a relationship," Valerie started slowly. "My ex had been cheating on me and, well, I found out and ended it."

"Oh, I am so sorry to hear that."

"It's alright, we weren't meant to be."

"That's good dear, keep your head up. You know, Amelia is single too," Aunt Kennedy said.

I should have warned her, Amelia winced. "I found more champagne!" She called out to spare Valerie and herself, and as if to hide the fact that she had been listening. As she came into the parlor room, she saw that Valerie was blushing, and of course Aunt Kennedy was the picture of innocence.

When it was time for the ceremony to begin, Valerie left to get some photos of the groom and the crowd. Aunt Kennedy looked lovely. She was a timeless beauty; she wore her grey hairs like each was a jewel in her crown. She was radiant.

"You know," she said once Jason made his way over to them, "I am very lucky to have my happily ever after." She cupped both Jason's and Amelia's face with maternal affection. "I hope the same for each of you."

The music began. A crowd of about twenty people had gathered and went over to their seats. Valerie had quickly set up a tripod at the end of the aisle to record the party walking down and was crouched off-center at the altar. Amelia saw the man who Aunt Kennedy agreed to marry standing in a tan suit with a soft orange pocket square. He was bald, which surprised her and had kind eyes.

Amelia and Jason walked down the aisle together. Amelia was on Aunt Kennedy's side and Jason stood behind the groom. "I want to see the two important men in my life, with my best girl by my side." Aunt Kennedy had said.

When she walked down the aisle, Rhett had tears in his eyes and Aunt Kennedy was a bundle of laughter and joy. She looked like she could not stop smiling if she tried.

After the ceremony, there was food and music for dancing. Amelia went up to Valerie with a plate of chicken salad, tossed with cranberry raisins, walnuts, strawberries, avocado, and feta. "The balsamic is really sweet," Amelia held up the plate. "You need to eat something."

"I don't want to miss anything," Valerie protested, snapping photo after photo.

"Maid-of-honor duties include making sure the photographer doesn't overwork herself beyond hunger."

Valerie gave her a look. "You just made that up."

Amelia shrugged and hooked her arm in Valerie's. "Fine," Valerie said, "Thank you."

"Are you having a good time?" Amelia asked.

"I am. I love weddings. I haven't been to one since my cousin got married, which admittedly wasn't super fun because it was a Catholic wedding and there was a lot of subtle commentary on 'the sanctity of marriage' and 'God's intention for marriage'." Valerie chuckled, "Which basically means the rest of the family was waiting for me to react to the homophobic rhetoric."

"Did you?" Amelia asked.

Valerie shook her head. "I do not need to convince people that their opinions are wack."

Amelia laughed. Hard. Threw her head back and laughed so loudly that people at the tables around them paused momentarily to look. "I am sorry, I did not expect you to say 'wack'. Who says that anymore?"

Valerie laughed with her. "I guess we do."

"That's pretty wack," Amelia said.

"Very wack."

They giggled together and Valerie placed her hand on Amelia's thigh. In the moment, Amelia could not tell if it was just a happenstance or if it was flirtatious. How many moments with Valerie were flirtatious? How many were in her head?

Amelia feared giving an undue amount of importance into the little moments that could either mean everything or mean nothing.

The sound of clinking glass broke her train of thought. Aunt Kennedy was standing to make a speech. Valerie picked up her camera and moved to take some photos, leaving Amelia at the table alone.

"Hello everyone!" She owned the spotlight. "I am going to make a little speech tonight on behalf of myself and my husband. I will never get tired of calling him my husband," she laughed. "Our story started many years ago, although I will not say how long. I know I look a lot younger than I am, so I will keep the ambiguity going," another laugh rolled through the crowd.

"There were a lot of years and a lot of life that we had in between our beginning and today. A lot of time apart. With different loves in different cities, and I know that neither of us regret the lives we've lived, the loves we've had. I am thankful that we reconnected before the end, and that we can spend our futures together as friends and lovers." The crowd applauded as the couple kissed.

Amelia thought about Aunt Kennedy's speech as they cut the cake, the workers in their polo shirts passing out plates to each table. Amelia knew that Aunt Kennedy was right about not regretting the in-between years, but she could not help but feel sad too. She did not want to spend her life waiting for someone to connect with at the end of her life. She wanted to have the in-between years too.

Valerie was taking photos of the couple as they fed each other a bite of wedding cake. She was laughing with them, capturing it all on camera. One day, they'd look through these photos and remember how they finally made it back to each other.

I want to be able to look back at my life and see you, Amelia thought as she watched Valerie walk back over to the table.

"Do you want to dance?" Amelia asked.

Valerie held out her hand and smiled, "Yes."

They went over to the dance floor. There was a Mirrorball above them and a thousand string lights. The DJ was playing some 80's pop song. Amelia put her hands on Valerie's hips, and Valerie wrapped her hands behind Amelia's neck. They twisted their hips in time to the music, laughing all the while. Amelia spun Valerie around and for a while, nothing else existed. Nothing else mattered. It was just the music, the lights, and *her*. The music ended and the DJ asked everyone to clear the floor for the first dance of the bride and groom.

"Oh, one second," Amelia said, and she adjusted Valerie's necklace so the clasp would be in the back. She noticed that the pendant was that of a sand dollar.

Husband and wife took to the dance floor. The DJ started playing *It's Witchcraft* by Frank Sinatra. As Valerie swooped around to snap some photos, Amelia saw Groom whispering the lyrics in Aunt Kennedy's ear, their bodies leaning against one another as they swayed slowly; lost in their own moment.

After the wedding, Amelia drove Valerie back to her hotel. The drive was quiet, both women exhilarated and exhausted from the day.

"I will have the photos edited as soon as I can," Valerie said. "I'm not sure how long it'll take exactly."

"No worries, whenever you get to it." Amelia replied. The silence felt like it was holding its breath. It wasn't uncomfortable, but it was electric. "Thank you, again, so much for coming to the rescue. You really saved the day."

"Thank you! I had a great time. Kennedy and Rhett are so sweet."

"Yeah, they are." Amelia said.

Silence again. So many words that could be said, but Amelia wasn't sure how to say them. *How do you tell a girl that she's beautiful without sounding like a creep?* She wondered.

"And I am glad I got to spend some time with you," Valerie said. "Outside of the theatre."

Amelia felt herself smile, "I am glad too, who else would've been my dance partner?"

"Jason, probably," Valerie chuckled.

"Yeah, but Jason isn't as pretty as you," Amelia said. *Shit, did I just say that?*

"Thank you," Valerie said. "You looked amazing tonight too." Then after a moment, "Not that you do not always look amazing," Valerie started to ramble.

Amelia laughed as she pulled up to the hotel. "Thank you."

They sat in the car for an extended moment, Amelia wasn't sure if she should try and kiss her. It wasn't really a date, but it wasn't *not* a date, right? *No, she was technically working. You need to ask her on an actual date and everyone involved needs to know it's a date in order for it to be a date.* "I will see you tomorrow?" she said instead.

"Yeah," Valerie smiled, "Tomorrow." She got out of the car and released her hair from her claw clip, the black waves covering the aquamarine, as she walked into the hotel.

Amelia drove away thinking about that little sand dollar necklace and how it felt when they danced together.

Chapter 16

At rehearsal the following week, Amelia had decided to focus on the acting in a few moments that weren't coming across as strongly as she would like. Specifically, the scene where the wolf was stalking Little Red. The actors who were playing Little Red and Jack were the only people in the cast who were still in high school, although they were both eighteen years old, and the actor playing the Wolf was nervous about making Little Red uncomfortable.

The Wolf was holding back, and Red was a newer actor. Amelia was hoping that if she got the wolf comfortable with laying on the creepiness thicker, then Red would be able to reciprocate the energy.

"Here is what we are going to do," Amelia said once both performers were on stage, "Wolf, I want you to get as close as you can to Red without touching her. And I mean a hair away. And Red, I want you to be oblivious that he's so close for a good portion of the song. Don't look at him until he grabs the basket. Okay?"

The actors nodded and began the scene. Valerie captured some photos of The Wolf stalking Little Red Riding Hood. They ran through the scene again, this time, Dylan was more animated, he got closer to Little Red, inside of her bubble without touching her. It was perfectly gross, and it made Valerie's skin crawl.

Which was the desired effect.

"How did that run feel?" Amelia asked. Both actors nodded emphatically. "It was perfect. Let's all take fifteen? Take bathroom breaks and drink water. Then, we are going to run this one more time after the break and have our circle."

"Thank you fifteen!" The cast chorused back.

Valerie loved the way theatre people were. The lingo, the understanding; every show was like being a limb to a living organism that was brought into being by all its moving parts. And then dismantled and dispersed into new beings repeatedly. Having never been part of a theatre community before, she was enjoying the process. And the little things, like the "thank you fifteen" call and response, really showed how everyone worked together. Even more, she was impressed at how much people dedicated to this without pay. One hundred percent volunteer-based cast.

During the fifteen-minute break, Amelia ran backstage to check on the dressing rooms. She thought of it as a safety sweep, just to make sure lights weren't falling out of the ceiling and people weren't climbing pyramids made of swivel chairs. These sweeps also helped her feel the energy of the cast. If she walked in on fighting or tense behavior, she could nip it in the bud, but she couldn't deal with it if she didn't know about it. That was just Amelia's opinion.

Meanwhile, Valerie walked into the pit. The orchestra pit was the flat area in front of a stage, where a live band could sit to play for the show, with the conductor looking at the performance to guide them. She opened the camera app on her phone. Some of the actors were sitting in the corner of the stage, having a conversation with someone else in the wings. But two of the ensemble girls were in the middle of the stage practicing their dance for one of the songs. Valerie took a short video of the girls doing the ballroom choreography.

"Hey! Do you mind doing a sequence quick for a behind the scenes video?" she asked them.

"Sure!" they replied. At hearing this, a few others of the cast came forward to also be in the video.

"We'll take it from the ballroom scene. The first night at the ball," said the shorter of the two original girls.

And just like that, magic. They were all dancing the same moves, even without music. One boy in the wings started playing the accompaniment from his phone. Valerie caught it all on film; the simple joy of doing what they loved, even for an audience of one.

Unnoticed, Amelia had come back. The power tools were still securely locked in the workshop and the cast had been both safe and happy. She had seen Valerie invite the cast to practice for some footage.

It had been so long since she had been on stage, even in the wings, during a performance or rehearsal. She had been directing or working the technical side shows… And there was that magical feeling in the air of watching a moment come to life.

She looked at Valerie, focused as she captured the dancers on film. She wondered how Valerie could truly be so utterly unaware of how captivating she was.

The dance ended. "Great job!" Valerie said. "I mean, I am not a professional like Amelia, but you guys look great!"

Amelia stood in the wings, hidden, a little longer. Valerie was playing the footage back for the ensemble, who were all nodding their heads in approval and excitement. If only there was more time, if only Valerie did not have to live so far, if only she did not have a whole career and home in Seattle, if only Amelia could ask her to stay…

There was something like a spark there. She felt it, warming up her insides and melting away the walls she had fought so hard to build. Valerie was affecting her so deeply and neither seemed to notice or be trying.

When Valerie looked up, they made eye contact. Amelia wanted to look away but held the gaze. Valerie smiled, and Amelia felt her smile widen in return.

V, you have no idea what you are doing to me, Amelia thought.

Once the crowd had dispersed, Jason called out "Five minutes!" to which everyone else – including Valerie – replied, "Thank you, five!"

Amelia was going towards Valerie but someone else had beaten her there. Then Paige, who Valerie remembered was playing Cinderella, came over to where Valerie was posting the video she had just filmed. Amelia kept walking over to Jason, hoping that it wasn't obvious that she had changed directions so abruptly.

"Hey Valerie," she said.

"Hi, Cinderella," Valerie said, picking up the habit of switching between actor and character names, "What's up?"

Paige looked a little nervous, fidgeting with the charm bracelet on her wrist. Valerie noticed the large single diamond on her left hand.

"Is everything okay?" Valerie tried again, wondering what Paige could possibly need from her and not Amelia.

"Yes," Paige said. Then she did a short exhale, like she was stealing herself to do something. "I need to ask you for a favor, or, not a favor, but for help. Wait, no," she shook her head. "Sorry. I don't have the right words right now. Let me try again."

Valerie waited, giving Paige a moment to collect herself and try again.

"My husband and I are looking for someone to work with us before deployment. We haven't really had a chance before, I mean, he looked into a few but ultimately it has been me looking for someone. To be honest, I would prefer a woman because I feel more comfortable, you know?" Paige looked at her hopefully.

"Uh," Valerie started, taken aback. "What exactly are you asking me? Because it sounds like something very inappropriate."

Paige looked confused. "Family photos?"

Valerie laughed a huff of relief. "Ha! Paige, you should've started with that!"

"Didn't I?"

"No," Valerie continued laughing. "You made it sound like you were looking for a third."

Paige blushed scarlet, "Ohmygod, I am so sorry."

"It's alright. Yes, I would love to take photos for you guys."

Paige smiled warmly, which brightened her features after the initial embarrassment. "Thank you so much, Valerie! I don't have rehearsal on Tuesday; how about then?"

"Sure, we can meet here and get some golden hour photos."

"Places!" Jason called out.

"Thank you, places!" replied Paige instinctively.

"You have my number? Message me and we can set something up," Valerie said.

Valerie walked over to the third row and sat right next to Amelia.

"Anyone sitting here?" Valerie asked jokingly.

Amelia shook her head and invited her to sit down. "Can I see what you were filming?" she asked.

"Of course," Valerie said as she opened the video on her phone. The smell of copal and honey radiated from her. Amelia resisted the urge to ask what perfume or lotion she used. It was sweet and comforting; it smelt like sunshine and soft blankets.

"That looks really good," Amelia said, because she had to say something to distract her from how amazing Valerie smelt. *God, who fangirls over how someone smells?* She wondered.

"Thanks, I think the trees came out great. You were definitely right about the fabric leaves," Valerie said. "It makes it much more dynamic."

"Thank you," she said. Valerie acknowledging her idea and then complimenting it weeks later… It was nice to know that she had been listening. "Alright everyone!" Amelia called out, "Let's run from the top of Act 2! Call for lines if you need to, Jason is on book."

The act started and Valerie pulled out her camera and worked on her computer, occasionally looking up to watch the rehearsal. Or more accurately, to watch Amelia.

Amelia had planned to write notes on any scenes she would need to workshop later in the week. She meant to write down a list of any songs that needed to be revisited with the vocal director. She had planned to be a very focused, very productive director. But Amelia had a hard time focusing on anything other than the little bit of space between her knee and Valerie's.

INTERMISSION

Playlist:

- *Strawberry Mentos* – Leanna Firestone
- *Perfect Places* – Lorde
- *The 1* – Taylor Swift
- *Strawberry Blonde* – Chloe Moriondo
- *Madison* – Orla Gartland
- *Pancakes for Dinner* – Lizzy McAlpine
- *Crush* – Tessa Violet
- *Underground* – Cody Fry
- *Would You Be So Kind* – Dodie
- *Valerie* – Mark Ronson ft. Amy Winehouse
- *To the Bone* – Sammy Copley
- *Sweet Creature* – Harry Styles
- *Daylight* – Taylor Swift

Act Two

"No knot unties itself."
- Mysterious Man from *Into the Woods*

"I just think that you are what you love."
- Taylor Swift, "Daylight"

Chapter 17

At the next rehearsal, Valerie continued interviewing various cast members. She thought about interviewing the characters of Baker and Baker's Wife together, but since the actors for Baker and Witch were married in real life, she thought it was more fun to have them be a dynamic duo. She had set up the camera in the lobby, so the concession booth was behind the interviewee.

"To take a line from your character, Ariel, you two make a *lovely couple*," Valerie said.

"Aww thank you," Ariel said.

"We are really excited to be able to do this show as a family," Adam added, kissing his wife's hairline. "Our baby isn't even here yet and they're already in a musical!"

After the couple, Valerie asked Austin for an interview.

Austin sat down across from her, he was wearing a black button up shirt with white music notes on it, unbuttoned with a navy-blue shirt underneath. His short blonde hair was styled with the normal loose curls. Valerie could understand why Jason was pinning after him, his sun-kissed skin, his sparkling blue eyes, and Valerie could see Austin's toned arms.

"Hey, Austin, you ready?" Valerie asked. He took a sip of water and nodded, crossing a knee over his ankle. "Great, let's get started. First question, what brought you to The Rose Theatre?"

"Well, I was acting here before it was The Rose, back before the pandemic. I've known Amelia and Jason for a long time. They're good people." Austin had that dazzling celebrity talk show guest smile. He was charisma in human form.

"How did you know them?" Valerie asked.

"Oh, school, you know." Austin said, and Valerie could feel that he didn't want to talk about it. Valerie was curious about the history between Jason and Austin but had to stay focused on the questions at hand, and not a moment too soon. Jason had come in behind Austin and was looking over something on his clipboard. Valerie had a feeling that Jason was trying to watch inconspicuously.

"Give me a pitch, why should people come see *Into the Woods*?"

Austin was comfortable again, the ease from before settling over him. "*Into the Woods* is a beautiful recreation of so many fairy tales and maintaining the feel of a cohesive story. All the while, it covers so many ways people have to overcome adversity and grow into themselves."

Valerie thought it looked like Jason wasn't breathing. "That's great, final question, what's your favorite moment in the show that you are not in?"

Austin laughed, "You had to put that qualifier on there?"

"So many people were saying your duet *Agony* is their favorite!"

Austin beamed, "My favorite part is when Emily, who plays the Baker's Wife, is reeling after our, uh, interaction," he gave a sheepish smile. "When she realizes that the best thing for herself and her life is the man who has always been by her side. It really moves me."

Jason disappeared into the office. "That was great, Austin, thank you."

"Of course," he stood up to leave, "and thank you, for doing all this. I know it's your job, but I've been watching all the posts online and I think you're doing a great job. I know it means a lot to, uh, everyone."

Valerie packed up her camera. "I'm happy to help."

"Can I ask you something?"

"Sure," Valerie started putting away her tripod. Austin looked around a little nervously. "Is everything okay?"

Just then, a few cast members came out into the lobby to grab water bottles from behind the concession stand. Emily came up to Austin and he walked away with her.

"A bunch of people are going to see *Pippin* tomorrow," Amelia told Valerie after dismissing the cast. She had a messy bun with small sections pulled out to frame her face. "So… do you want to go with me?"

Valerie smiled, "Like a date?"

Amelia blushed, "It's not *not* a date? But most of the cast will be there."

Valerie tucked one of the sections of hair behind Amelia's ear, "I look forward to it. I'll pick you up?"

"Jason, you are not helping." Amelia was pacing around her room trying on different outfits. "V is going to be here soon."

Jason was on video chat; he was also primping for the night. "Wear the blue one."

Amelia put on the blue blouse again. It had a v-neck and butterfly sleeves. She paired it with a pair of black business pants. "It feels too 'business bitch' and not 'single and ready to mingle', right?"

"Yeah, but this is also a business night for you, right? What if we need to borrow set pieces or costumes? We want to foster a strong relationship with the other theatres in the area," Jason said.

"That's true. At least we'll both be there," Amelia started picking up the clothes she had spread across the room.

"Actually, I'm not going."

"What? But you've been getting ready this whole time?"

"Yeah, I have a date."

Amelia grabbed her phone and shook it as if she was shaking him, "You didn't tell me?"

105

Jason laughed with faux mania, "Love you, gotta go, bye!"

Her home screen returned to her phone as the call ended. Amelia was going to call him back, but saw a text from Valerie.

V: *I'm outside!*

A: *Okay, be right out.*

Then she sent a separate message over to Jason.
A: *I'll need DETAILS.*

J: *:)*

Amelia slid into the passenger seat of Valerie's car.
"You look amazing, Ames."
"You do too."
Valerie was wearing the split color top that she wore to Aunt Kennedy's wedding. "Thanks, I only had so many outfits packed." She laughed sheepishly.
"What do you know about *Pippin*?" Amelia asked.
Valerie thought briefly. "Wasn't there a circus movie about it or something?"
"Yes and no. I would suggest listening to the album on the way, but I think you should go in blind instead."
"Whatever you say, boss. Who's all going tonight?"
Amelia listed them on her fingers, "Adam and Ariel, Paige and her husband, I think Emily and Austin, too. A few people. Not Jason though."
"Not Jason?"
"He had other plans, I guess."
Just then, the phone rang. Amelia could see on the display screen of Valerie's car she was getting an incoming call from Jorge.
"Sorry, I need to take this," Valerie said, hitting the accept call button.
"Hi, this is Valerie."

An annoyed male voice came through, "Hey Val, how's it going? Good? Good. So, I was looking through the file. You really need to step it up. I just don't think these are up to my standard of quality, and since this client will eventually come back to my desk, I want to make sure I don't have to start from scratch."

Amelia opened her mouth to argue, but Valerie shook her head. Jorge kept talking.

"Look, I know it's your first-time taking photos, but maybe you could look at my stuff and just do your best to emulate that, okay? Okay, great. Talk to you later, keep trying your best."

The call ended, and Amelia noticed the way Valerie's grip had tightened on the steering wheel.

"That guy is a total dick," Amelia said. Valerie hadn't relaxed her hands. "You're doing great, V."

"He's so frustrating. He acts like I've never used a camera before, I just… I don't want to think about it."

They arrived at Limelight Theatre and made their way to their seats. Amelia noticed that Valerie was more withdrawn than usual. She had busied herself by reading the program. The show began and all through Act 1, Amelia fought the urge to hold Valerie's hand. As the lights rose for intermission, she leaned over.

"V, are you okay?"

"Oh yeah, but I have so many questions about this show."

"I was worried about earlier, in the car," Amelia said, placing a comforting hand on her shoulder.

Valerie smiled, "I'm okay, Ames. This show has been a great distraction."

Act 2 went by quickly. Amelia and Valerie had a great time and said goodbye to their friends.

"I feel like Pippin really goes through the seven deadly sins," Amelia said on their way back. They were listening to the album and discussing the show. "That's how I would direct it."

"I'm a little confused about the leading player, and his girlfriend is just another actor?" Valerie said, "She's not really Catherine? It feels so, oh what's that movie, the one where everything is filmed and Jim Carrey's character is the only one who doesn't know it's all a set?"

"That's *The Truman Show*. And it can be done either way."

Before they knew it, they were sitting outside Amelia's apartment.

"This was fun," Amelia said.

"Thanks for inviting me."

"Of course." Amelia looked up at her lonely apartment. Valerie failed to successfully stifle a yawn. "I should probably go inside," Amelia said, opening the car door, "I would just sit in here and talk all night."

"Sorry, I'm super tired. I had a photoshoot with Paige and her husband this morning. It's been a long day."

"Of course, good night."

Amelia flopped into bed and listened to the echoing emptiness of her apartment and fell asleep thinking about Valerie.

Chapter 18

In the dim light of Valerie's hotel room early on Saturday morning, Valerie's phone lit up.

A -   *Want some more behind the scenes?*

Valerie smiled and bit her lip in thought before replying.

V -   *Sure, what's on the calendar?*

A -   *Costume organizing.*
        Dinner first? At Grill and Vine, it's a bar by
The Rose.
        7pm?

V -   *Okay!*

Valerie paced around her room, picking out which outfit to wear. Since she had most of the day to kill, she opened the curtains and decided to video chat her mom.

"Hi!" her mom answered, smiling. "How's California?" Elizabeth Ross was wearing her purple reading glasses and her short hair framed her face.

"It's good," Valerie said. "I have a few hours of free time and I was lonely."

"I have a three-day weekend next week," her mom said, "maybe I can come down and hang out with you."

Valerie smiled. "I would love that. There's a crystal shop right next to a used bookstore that we can go to. They have opalite."

"Yes, absolutely. I will fly down after work on Friday. I just need to make sure that Faith can check on the cats. Although it should be fine. She's a good neighbor."

Faith was the elderly next-door neighbor at Elizabeth's condo. The cats would go from Elizabeth's to Faith's, back and forth. For an unknown amount of time, they were eating four meals a day, until Elizabeth noticed the cat's considerable weight gain, and Faith realized these strays were very well fed and well taken care of. Once the women had discovered the feline master plan, they agreed that Faith would feed them treats each day around noon, but their breakfasts and dinners would be at Elizabeth's.

"So, are you okay? Do you need money or anything?"

"No mom, I'm okay."

"Just checking, baby."

"What's new with you?" Valerie prompted.

Elizabeth started explaining the latest gossip from her coworkers. "So, we are getting a new principal. I think the district figured out that she couldn't cut it."

"That's good; you didn't like her."

Elizabeth harrumphed. "No one likes her. Our mascot is the Stars. She keeps saying 'Good morning, Rockets!' because the last school she was at were the Rockets. Like, come on, it's not hard to say the right name. It's been months."

Valerie had to agree with that. After a few more minutes of conversation, Elizabeth said, "Well, I need to go. Faith and I are having dinner together. A girl's night."

"Sounds fun, Mom."

As the hours passed by, Valerie compiled a few posts and sent them over to Matt. Since the confrontation with Mr. Packet, she had decided to keep her boss updated about every detail. She also shared a link to the file that held everything on The Rose Theatre, not just the highlights. In total, she had hundreds of photos, but only a dozen of each were up to par with her standards.

She still had three hours before she had to meet Amelia, so she decided to edit the photos she had taken of Paige.

Valerie sat comfortably at the desk in the hotel room, with *Gilmore Girls* playing on the television in the background.

Paige's husband, Lance Corporal Moore was not how Valerie expected him to be. He wasn't the super tough guy marine that came to mind. He was shy. He deflected every photo to Paige. He would turn to her at the last minute even when she was looking at the camera. It was obvious that she was the light of his world.

It made some really sweet and beautiful photos. The love was palpable. They had brought a change of clothes with them so there were two sets of photos. The first set had Lance Corporal Moore in his green cammies while Paige wore a light blue sundress. When someone was in uniform, the photos always came out patriotic. The second set, he was in civilian clothes, jeans, and a grey Henley shirt. She wore leggings and a blouse. The session had been a lot of fun for the second set, not as emotional as the first. Moore had made Paige laugh with abandon, and Valerie's favorite photo was of Paige laughing with her head back, holding Moore's hand while he openly admired her.

Time slipped away. Valerie finished editing the photos and uploaded them to a cloud where she could share them with Paige. She looked at the little clock on the corner of her laptop screen and saw that it was 6:30 P.M. She had fifteen minutes to be at the bar!

She threw on black overalls over the tie-dye peach and cream t-shirt she had slept in, slipped on her black converse, grabbed her wallet and phone then rushed out the door.

Luckily, the bar Amelia suggested was only a five-minute drive away, and she was able to find parking easily enough. Crossing two intersections, Valerie arrived only slightly out of breath. Amelia was waiting for her outside on the curb. She was wearing a sage colored sleeveless crop top and capri length grey leggings.

They sat down and ordered a bottle of Riesling and a mozzarella and veggie pizza.

"Do you believe in soul mates?" Amelia asked.

Valerie almost missed her mouth with her drink. "Wow, we're really getting right to it, aren't we?"

"It's just a question," Amelia laughed. "Do you believe there's one person for everyone?"

Valerie thought for a moment, eating a stray bell pepper slice from her plate.

"I think," she started slowly, "yes."

"Really?"

"Yeah, I mean, I don't think there's just *one* person for every person. The odds of a one-to-one ratio... it's impossible."

"That's not very romantic of you," Amelia said. "I think there are soul mates. I think you find the right person when you're meant to."

"I don't disagree," Valerie said. "But it's like the timing and the person have to match up, so what if you meet 'the one', but too early?"

"Right person, wrong time?" Amelia suggested, taking a sip of her wine.

"Right! But then you meet someone else, and it's the right person at the right time, does that mean the first person was never the right person?"

"No... wait, yes?" Amelia hesitated.

"It gets muddy. But I think there are multiple soul mates for each person. One might be the best friend in your life, they are a soul mate even though it's not romantic. Or they might be the person who changes you for the better, even though you only knew them a short while. And of course, there's the person you spend most of your life with, who is a romantic partner..." Valerie trailed off. "If you're asking me if I believe that there's someone like that for me, then my answer is – I hope so."

Amelia reached out and held Valerie's hand to offer comfort, but when they locked eyes, the spark between them lit a flame. They both quickly let go. Valerie took a sip of her wine and Amelia grabbed a slice of pizza.

Should I ask and clarify if this is a date? Valerie wondered.

"So is this-"

"I'm really-" Amelia started at the same time. "Sorry, go ahead."

"I just, uh," Valerie chuckled weakly, "I forgot what I was going to say. You go ahead." Valerie took a sip of wine to hide the fact she was lying through her teeth.

"I'm really glad that you're here," Amelia said. Valerie felt her body warm in response. "Like, professionally." Amelia said quickly. "It's really nice to have a partner of sorts to work on things with."

"Oh, right." Valerie said.

"You're a real asset," Amelia continued. "And more than that, too. You've really grown on me."

"Yeah, I'm, uh, really happy that SPRUCE sent me out here."

Amelia took a drink and drained the remainder of the wine in her glass. Valerie tried not to notice the way her shoulders gave a slight shake as she swallowed.

"What I'm really trying to say is that you are becoming someone who is very important to me."

"Professionally?" Valerie asked.

Amelia held her eye contact intently, and after a beat, gave a slight shake of her head, her soft red waves barely swaying.

Valerie slid her forearm across the table, palm up. Amelia placed her own hand in Valerie's and breathed a sigh of relief when Valerie's thumb and forefinger gave her a gentle squeeze.

The waitress, who was bustling from table to table came by and asked if they were ready to cash out their bill.

"Sure," Amelia went to grab her wallet, but Valerie had her beat, pulling her debit card out of the chest pocket of her overalls. "I got it."

"No, I invited you, which means I pay," Amelia said, still trying to find her wallet inside her tote bag.

"You snooze you lose," Valerie teased.

The waitress hesitated for a only a moment, then took Valerie's card and completed the transaction on a wireless card reader she wore on her hip.

"Thank you, ladies. Have a great evening!"

Amelia pointed a finger at Valerie as the waitress walked away, "I'm buying next time."

Valerie just shrugged, "I'm not keeping score, Ames."

They drove separately back over to the hotel to drop off Valerie's car, then Amelia parked in front of the theatre.

As she unlocked the door, Amelia said, "We have some champagne in the office, if you want to have some."

"Sure," Valerie said.

"Can you grab some cups from concessions?"

As Valerie made her way back in the dim light of the lobby, her steps echoing, she felt a shiver run up her spine.

"It's kind of creepy in here by yourself," Valerie said, putting two red plastic cups on the table in the office

"You know," Amelia said, "almost every theatre has a ghost." She poured them equal amounts of champagne, which ended up being most of the bottle.

"Does The Rose have a ghost?" Valerie asked, her tone playful.

"Oh sure," Amelia mused. "I'm still working on her story, though. That's how you make a good ghost- they've all got great stories. Something memorable. No one ever talks about it, but I think this is how all urban legends are born."

"I think this ghost is a man," Valerie said, feeding into the bit.

Amelia smiled as they continued to make their way over to the green room backstage, and the costume loft door behind it.

114

"That works. I don't want a child ghost, because that would just end up in poltergeist territory."

"Like the movie?" Valerie held the door open for Amelia to climb up the stairs first.

"I don't know, I've never seen the movie."

"What?" Valerie was incredulous.

"I don't like scary things," Amelia shrugged, turning on the table lamps in the costume loft, filling the space with a soft orange light.

"But you want to fabricate a ghost story in a dark theatre at night?"

Amelia shrugged. "I'm not scared here, and I'm safe with you, right?"

Valerie blushed.

"I think his name should be Herbert." Amelia said this so matter of fact-ly that it made Valerie laugh. "What? It's obviously an outdated name."

"And Herbert was a surfer, he went by Bert and never Herb."

"Yes, that's perfect!"

Valerie started shifting through a collection of coats and capes on a metal rack. None of the hangers matched and the rack was overstuffed. A good problem to have, but definitely tedious to dig through.

"He had to have died in the building though, or else why would his ghost be here?" Amelia said.

Valerie thought. "Well, I don't think a violent death."

"Maybe he's just kind of a huge theatre lover?"

"Yes!" Amelia practically cheered. "He'd spend his days in the surf, his nights on the stage."

"The biography writes itself," Valerie said. "Hey, what about this one?" she attempted to pull out what looked like it might be a nice cloak for the witch. She was unaware that the wire hanger had hooked on a broken plastic hanger next to it and her hand flung back. Valerie lost her balance and fell onto a pile of clothes on the floor. Amelia laughed and plopped next to her, then took a swig of her drink. She had the most beautiful lips Valerie had ever seen. Full, plump, with the softest small curve at her cupid's bow. Valerie wondered what it would be like to taste the champagne off that soft curve.

Amelia looked at Valerie. They each saw each other, saw the other look at their lips.

"I really want to kiss you," Amelia took Valerie's hand, emboldened by the moment. "And I know that you just got out of a relationship, and if all this ends up being is some anecdote one day, then so be it. But I... I can't keep doing this. I can't keep wanting you like this. Of not knowing. I just want to know..." Amelia looked at her with those bright blue eyes.

Valerie did not want to wait any longer either. She took a piece of Amelia's hair and tucked it behind her ear. "Amelia," she breathed. They were closer, their noses touching slightly.

The tension was sizzling around them, Amelia swore she could hear it buzzing, no... vibrating. Then she understood that the vibration wasn't just her nerves turned up to eleven, but that it was coming from Valerie's pocket. Amelia pulled back slightly, thinking Valerie would check her phone.

Then it stopped suddenly, the incoming call going to voicemail. The room was quiet.

So quiet, that Amelia wondered if Valerie could hear her heart thudding in her chest. Valerie's right hand came up and her fingers gingerly curled around the back of Amelia's neck. They started to lean in again, when *buzz buzz buzzzz.*

Valerie put her forehead to Amelia's and let out an exhale. "I should probably get that."

Amelia bit her lip to keep herself from letting out a small whimper in protest.

Valerie stood up, and the spell was broken. As she pulled her phone out of her pocket answering, "Hey, Mom," as she walked down the stairs to have her conversation. Amelia went to the other side of the room and started clearing off a shelf and organizing shoes.

By the time Valerie returned, Amelia was in full worker mode, and Valerie recognized Amelia's musical theatre playlist blaring from her speakers.

"Everything okay?"

"Yeah, she was just telling me that she's going to come visit next weekend and she got the plane tickets."

"Nice."

Valerie looked at the pile of clothes that she and Amelia had been laying on just moments before. Amelia had managed to put away most of it; the pile was a third of its previous size.

"Sorry for the interruption."

"That's okay," Amelia said, blushing. "It's probably for the best anyway. Don't want to embarrass Bert."

"Of course not," Valerie said, playing along.

"Do you mind going through these racks of clothes and pulling the empty hangers? Any that look broken can go in the recycling."

"Sure," Valerie said, moving over to the racks.

"He was an actor too," Amelia said.

"Huh?" Valerie said, distracted.

"The ghost."

Valerie nodded, "Oh, right."

They worked for a while, singing along to songs as they came on. After making decent progress, they decided to call it a night.

"Thank you for helping me get this situated," Amelia said. "It's been one of those things that was just weighing on me to get done."

"Sure, and again, I'm sorry about my mom calling," Valerie started.

"Oh, don't apologize for that."

"Because I wanted to," Valerie tried again.

Amelia smiled sheepishly. "Maybe another time." She locked the doors to the theatre, pulling them to confirm they had been closed. "I should go rest before skating tomorrow."

When she turned, Valerie stepped closer. She opened her arms.

Amelia stepped fully into Valerie's embrace, hiding her face in Valerie's shoulder.

She felt the soft brush of Valerie's lips on her temple.

"Have a good night, Ames," Valerie stepped back, but their hands ended up holding on. The cars drove by on Pacific Coast Highway, and the cool air was veiled in mist.

The colors of the streetlights were stretching along the asphalt. The headlights of the cars were coming and going.

Amelia pulled Valerie back into her, Valerie's hands wrapped around the sides of Amelia's waist, just above her hips, and Amelia's arms came up and around Valerie's neck. They were face to face, and someone at the stoplight was playing music in their car.

They stood there for a second, just for a second. The question was clear in Amelia's eyes, and Valerie closed the distance.

The world around them was a different plane of existence. This kiss, even just a soft peck, took them to a different dimension where no one else existed. When they pulled apart, there was a clarity in Valerie's eyes.

Condensation and mist were layering on her hair like dew, and Amelia wiped a bit of her lipstick off of Valerie's bottom lip.

"I'll see you tomorrow?" Amelia asked.

"Tomorrow." Valerie promised.

Chapter 19

By the time Valarie arrived at the local skate rink, about half the cast was still waiting in line. She felt like an outsider sometimes, unsure of when she was welcomed or when she forced herself in. Maybe it was an inability to read social cues. Maybe it was social anxiety. She thought about making conversation but didn't want to make them uncomfortable; they didn't seem to notice her anyhow.

She pulled out her phone to check some of the photos she had taken earlier at the theatre and tried out some of her presets on them.

"You made it!" said Jason.

"Sure did." Valerie replied.

"Are you ready for tech week?"

"To be honest, I'm not sure what I need to be ready for. For the most part, I'm doing some final pushes for social media campaigns. I tried to get us a segment on a local news station, but they just are showing some video footage I sent them rather than coming to a rehearsal for a live shoot."

"Tech weeks are… hard," Jason said. "It can be rough on everyone because it's crunch time. Costumes, lights, sound… all the finishing touches that make rehearsals feel like more than just rehearsal. It's like, 'oh shit, people are going to see this, and soon.' Then there's just the physical aspect of it too."

"From what I've seen, theatre is basically a sport."

Jason laughed. "Pretty much. Every show is different obviously. Tech is hard because actors might push themselves too hard and wear out their voices or exhaust themselves before opening night. It's almost always fine in the end, but it's something to be aware of."

After paying for some rental skates, Valerie made her way in. The inside of the building was small. The rink itself was made of wood, and seating wrapped around the bottom and one side of the rink. There was a random assortment of picnic tables. Most had red and blue tablecloths on them. The floor outside the rink was covered in that thin carpet that was often in movie theaters with a 1990's style pattern of once vibrant shapes and squiggly lines.

Valerie saw the cast in the back corner and made her way over there. The actor playing Jack was the center of attention as she arrived.

"Guys, seriously I do not know how to skate," he said. "I am going to fall!"

"Probably," said one of the ensemble girls. "I will help you."

The ensemble girl's attraction to Jack went unnoticed by many. She continued to try and get his attention as he kept professing that he had awful balance.

"We'll probably all fall at some point," said Cinderella's Prince, Valerie remembered his name was Austin. She thought about how Jason had history with Austin, but they barely even looked at each other. Was that intentional? Was the history sour?

"Just please do not get hurt, we are going into tech week tomorrow," Amelia's voice came from the rink. Everyone turned. "When did you get here?" different cast members exclaimed. Valerie just smiled.

"Hey, you," Amelia said once she made her way off the rink, through the cast, and onto the bench beside her.

"Hey," Valerie replied. "Love the outfit. You have your own skates?" Amelia was wearing a lilac muscle shirt, black leggings, and baby blue skates with light up purple wheels. In her hair was a silver scrunchie that matched her reflective fanny pack, which of course, was covered in enamel pins.

"Thanks! And yeah, skating is like my therapy. Well, not really. I go to therapy and that's my therapy, but skating is stress relief."

They watched Jack struggle to let go of the wall on the rink.

"Ready to hit it?" Amelia asked. She was practically glowing.

Valerie laughed, "Hit it?" she asked. Amelia laughed too.

"You know what I mean, come on." Amelia led Valerie out to the rink. They stayed just a bit inside the outer edge of the traffic. The little kids were in the center, while the faster experienced skaters were on the outer lanes of the rink. There were a few who would swerve through the crowd, sometimes backwards.

"They make me so nervous, especially that one," Valerie nodded her head to a teenage boy with headphones on who was skating backwards through the crowd and occasionally flipping around.

"He won't hit you, he's really good."

"I'm not nervous of him running into me, I'm nervous because I'm very likely to fall at the worst time, and then trip him. Plus, he has headphones in so he wouldn't be able to hear me fall."

"Okay, worry wort. Let's go."

Amelia was not the best skater, but she was competent enough to be clearly having a great time; honestly, she could have been the worst one on the rink and Valerie still would have been in awe.

"Alright," said a feminine robotic voice over the loudspeakers, "We have a special song request from the cast and crew of Rose Theatre, they say 'you'll know who you are', so here it is… Valerie!"

Just then, the song Valerie by Amy Winehouse started to play, and Amelia was holding her hand as they skated around the rink, in disco lights under a dozen mirror balls. Valerie was acutely aware of the moment slipping by and wished she could freeze the moment, to make it extend and be able to hold Amelia in this place. To see her eyes reflecting the light. To wear it like scented lotion, to pull it out and relive it throughout the day. She wished she had her camera set up to record this.

121

"Stop making a fool out of me," Amelia sang, "Why don't you come on over, Valerie."

Was this an original idea? Someone singing this song to her?

No.

In fact, Valerie had been bullied as a kid, other students would taunt her with the lyrics. But kids could be mean. And this was not mean.

But this? This experience with Amelia washed all other memories of this song away. The cast was all singing. *Oh, theatre kids,* Valerie thought. Her cheeks were getting sore from the goofy grin she had on her face, but she could not have stopped smiling if she tried.

The room was spinning as she skated around. She was trying so hard to absorb the moment, but each detail felt so fleeting; the lights were rotating, and she was skating so she couldn't even look at Amelia and study her face or commit her expression to memory.

So, she focused on the one thing that wasn't shifting – Amelia's hand in hers. Soft, strong, and *there*, their fingers interlocked. The pull of skating one way or another, the way Amelia's watch felt against her wrist. Their hands were about the same size. She remembered dancing at the wedding, the kiss last night, and every moment together, and in an instant she knew.

This was more than a crush.

This was more than a fling or a showmance, this was something all at once more real and intangible. This feeling was enough to build a home from scratch with your bare hands. This feeling was what kept the moon chasing the sun through the sky. The whole galaxy was aligned for this perfect moment. She didn't want to break it, but the anxiety and doubt crept in. *It's not real, everything ends.*

As the song ended, Valerie and Amelia ended up in the middle of the rink, hugging but no longer moving; their fingers still interlocked. "I am really, really happy you are here, V." Amelia whispered in her ear. Valerie felt her heart fill up like a hydrogen balloon.

"Me too, Ames." She replied.

Each gave the other hand a squeeze as if a promise. A placeholder for an unspoken confession that they could not yet voice.

Chapter 20

Valerie was grateful that her mom was coming so she could have some space from the theatre. In the hours after the skate night, she realized that things with Amelia were progressing so fast. She needed to step back just to figure out her own feelings. But mostly, she wanted a distraction. There was a risk of getting caught up in the whirlwind of the fall. She wanted to be logical about this.

Her mom wanted to rest before going shopping and seeing the sights, which meant reading by the pool. "When I was younger and lived in an apartment, I would spend every day of the summer by the pool with a book. I would read until I got too warm, then I'd jump in the pool for a few minutes, and then get back on the chair and read. And I would do that for a few hours or until your dad came home."

Valerie applied sunscreen to her arms and smiled. She loved when her mom talked about her dad. "What would he say about you reading all day?"

"Oh, he'd call me a menace to society or a degenerate. Then we would have dinner and I'd read some more while he worked on his truck."

Her mom got quiet then, lost in the memory. She grabbed her book, a mass market paperback historical romance. Valerie used to be embarrassed about the salacious cover art of her mother's reading material, but as she got older, she became more and more desensitized to it. Valerie, being her mother's daughter, grabbed a book too, a high fantasy epic, complete with multiple points of view and dragons.

To each their own.

"So how are you?" Elizabeth asked while cooling off in the pool. "We haven't really talked about the breakup."

Valerie shrugged. "I am alright. It was a long time coming."

"Sure," Elizabeth said gently, "but you guys were together for a long time too."

"Only eight months."

"Still."

She joined her mom in the pool. "There were so many walls already built up. It was more insulting than hurtful." Of course, it had still hurt, there's no way for it to have *not* hurt.

"Once a cheater, always a cheater." Elizabeth said with a disapproving shake of her head.

Valerie felt the urge to defend Stacy rise in her like a bad habit. "I don't know about that," she started. Elizabeth gave her a look and said, "Oh honey," in a way that really meant *you are so delusional.*

"I'm not defending her," Valerie said, closing her eyes so that she could think straight, "I am just saying that I hope people are capable of growth and change. Maybe even Stacy, but I won't be waiting around to find out."

Elizabeth gave a noncommittal shrug. Valerie watched as she picked up her novel to continue reading, but before she could remove her bookmark, and before she lost her nerve, Valerie spoke up.

"Actually, there's someone else that I am interested in."

"Details!" Elizabeth exclaimed, as she slammed her book closed with excitement.

Valerie told her mom about Amelia. How they met, the moment in the costume loft, at the skate rink, and so many other little moments. Her mom listened.

"But I just don't know what to do now." Valerie concluded. By this point, they had both migrated back into the water.

"What do you mean?" Elizabeth asked.

"Well, I know I'm going to be leaving soon, and I know that I already have a really full schedule trying to get my work done and doing photography on the side. And I know that she's really busy too." Valerie let out a frustrated groan. "And I should not be thinking about someone romantically when I just got out of a relationship."

"I am not sure if 'should not' is the right phrase." Elizabeth interjected. "You like her, you are both consenting adults."

"Yeah, but I don't want a showmance. I don't want to fall hard and fast and have it end up like Stacy." Valerie started.

"It's simple. As long as you are clear and communicative then I don't see what the problem is." Elizabeth said, ever the intellectual air sign.

Valerie shook her head. "I don't know if she wants a long-distance relationship. And no one wants to be a rebound."

"Who said it has to be a relationship? You're twenty-four years old, Valerie. And as far as I know, becoming a nun is not one of your aspirations. All I am saying is that you are allowed to have a good time for the time you are here. And so long as you are both upfront about what you want, then you know what to expect. Rebounds are fine."

"I... I really like her, Mom."

"What will be will be on its own. Release expectation. Release desire. Things will play out how they're supposed to."

After they were done by the pool, mother and daughter went to the crystal shop. Elizabeth bought opalite earrings for herself and a rose quartz heart for Valerie. Valerie found another enamel pin, one that said "un-phased" that had the moon cycle in a circle. Valerie could not resist. She bought it for Amelia. Elizabeth noticed and raised her brows inquisitively.

"Amelia really likes enamel pins. She collects them, they're all over her tote bag," Valerie said. Elizabeth pursed her lips together, but it did little to hide the knowing smile.

They went to the beach and the little coffee shop across from The Rose. "I want to try that panini you say is so good," Elizabeth tried to be nonchalant.

Valerie walked in a little nervous; she could not stop herself from looking around for Amelia's red hair. They ordered and sat down and Valerie had decided that Amelia must not be working a shift right then.

"There is the theatre," Valerie pointed to the building across the street.

"Oh, it's lovely," Elizabeth swooned.

"Good afternoon, ladies." They turned and there was Amelia, hair in a braid with a black bandana with white paisleys on top. Valerie's heart leapt and squeezed and inflated in her chest at the sight of her.

"Amelia!" she said a little too loudly, then laughed and even to her own ears it sounded forced. "This is my mom; Mom, this is Amelia."

Amelia stuck out her hand and Elizabeth shook it. "I've heard so much about you!" Valerie felt her cheeks warm. "And I love the theatre! Valerie was just pointing it out to me."

"Oh, thank you!" Pride lifted Amelia's chest. "It has definitely been a wild ride and I am excited about it. I could give you a tour if you'd like?"

"Absolutely!" Elizabeth beamed.

Valerie was embarrassed by her mom's forwardness. "I'm sure Ames is busy."

Amelia's lips curled into a smile when she noticed Valerie's embarrassment. It was funny and cute to see her trying so hard to be casual.

"Well, then let's get dinner," Elizabeth said. "I'd love to know more about the theatre and Valerie's friend."

Valerie looked at her, almost hopeful. She hoped Amelia would say yes, but also desperately wanted to avoid her mom playing matchmaker. Amelia held her gaze and there was a distinct twinkle in her eye as she accepted the invitation.

"She's cute," Elizabeth said when she and Valerie were back in the hotel room.

"Mmhmm." Valerie said.

"You mentioned that you did a photoshoot?" Elizabeth said.

"Yeah, two technically. Amelia called me for a wedding she was in and then someone in the show wanted photos with her husband before he deploys soon."

"Can I see them?"

Valerie showed her mom the pictures. As Elizabeth was scrolling through them, Valerie said, "I might have another photoshoot soon, I had a bunch of military spouses reaching out to me for their family photos thanks to Paige."

"That's amazing, honey."

"I had to turn most of them down because SPRUCE is my actual job right now. And I've been getting emails about stuff for other people's accounts."

Elizabeth's brows furrowed in concern, "Wait, have they still been sending you editorial things the whole time you've been here?"

"Yeah, but not so much. I had someone ask me to take a call for them the other day, but I was like, 'No, I'm with a client right now.' They haven't been bothering me too much, at least."

Elizabeth shook her head. "I don't like how they treat you sometimes. You need a different job."

Valerie shrugged. "I want to open my own photography business so bad, but it's too big of a risk."

Elizabeth closed the laptop and got up to go over to the bed. "Life without risk would be boring. But I raised you so that you've got a good head on your shoulders, and that you're prioritizing the need for stability. I think you could do it. If you had taken all the requests you got, you'd be able to really set yourself up."

Valerie didn't know what to say to that.

"I'm going to take a nap before dinner," Elizabeth said.

"Alright, I think I'm going to just read some more." Instead, Valerie stalked Amelia on social media. She looked through her posts and photos, song lyrics, backstage selfies, and when she scrolled far enough back, some really cringe theatre kid memes.

At dinner, Amelia wore a pale-yellow tank top with blue jean cut offs. She walked in and saw Valerie and Elizabeth at a tall round table in the middle of the dining area of a little Mexican restaurant called Te Amo. Valerie was wearing a cheetah print romper with her hair in space buns. Elizabeth wore a black t-shirt with red plaid pants and a fedora.

"I love the patterns," Amelia said.

"We go all out," Valerie said. She seemed more confident now.

Amelia sat on the tall chair. Elizabeth waited until she ordered a drink to ask, "How did you know you wanted to open a theatre?"

"Well, it's what I am passionate about. I love it and I believe that the arts are essential. When I saw the theatre was for sale... I don't know, it sounds really cheesy, but I think it was a sign from the universe." Amelia shook her head and grabbed her water for a sip. "That sounds crazy, but that's how it went."

Elizabeth adjusted her hat. "You know, I got a message from the universe when I was pregnant with Valerie."

"Here we go again," Valerie groaned half-heartedly.

"Really?" Amelia asked.

"Don't encourage her," Valerie said in a mock whisper.

"I was taking a shower after... you know... oh do not make that face, Valerie... and I had a vision of rainbows." She turned her attention to Amelia, "Her dad and I were trying to have a baby for a while and had a very early miscarriage. Lost them before I even knew I had them. But that day I saw rainbows when I closed my eyes. So, I looked it up! What do rainbows symbolize? Well of course in the Bible it's a promise from the Abrahamic god, and in Greek mythology it's Isis, a messenger goddess. And then I find out that having a baby after loss of pregnancy is called a rainbow baby. So here she is. My pot of gold at the end of the rainbow." Elizabeth caressed a lock of Valerie's hair with such tenderness that Amelia's heart squeezed at the sight of it. Not quite envy, but longing. Her own mother had been more interested in whatever fads were trending than caring for her own kids. Eccentric to the brim of neglect.

"Rainbows are also, obviously, a symbol of the queer community, so she likes to joke that her vision was prophetic. I was a lesbian before I was more than a clump of cells." Valerie teased.

Amelia laughed and almost shot water out of her nose.

"Anyway, can we move on? We are barely eating the chips and salsa and we are dangerously close to the 'naked baby photos' zone." Valerie said. "Instead, how about we talk about literally anything else."

"Are you seeing anyone?" Elizabeth asked Amelia.

"Oh my god," Valerie pinched her nose with her thumb and finger.

"I think you would be great friends with my Aunt Kennedy," Amelia laughed.

Valerie nodded, "Yes, you would."

They told Elizabeth about Aunt Kennedy's wedding. At one point, Amelia's hand landed on Valerie's forearm and the jolt of energy left her entire arm from wrist to shoulder tingling.

She saw her mom notice but pretended that nothing was affecting her in any way whatsoever.

"Did you grow up locally?" Elizabeth asked.

"Yes, but I moved after high school with my best friend to go to San Diego State. Then we both came back when we had graduated."

"What was your major?"

Amelia had a half smile, "Um, theatre, actually."

"Well, that makes sense," Elizabeth laughed. "I thought maybe business or something."

"Amelia also worked in medical billing," Valerie chimed in, "she's capable of success in different fields."

Amelia's cheeks warmed and she busied herself with eating another chip from the center of the table. Thankfully, the food arrived and once everyone was eating, the playful interrogation paused.

Valerie had been nervous of all the different ways this night would go, but those worries had dissolved. Amelia was somehow perfectly playing the "meet the parents" role, while still being entirely herself. Unlike when Stacy had met Elizabeth, and Valerie couldn't even recognize her.

"They don't have tacos like this in Washington," Elizabeth said. "I'll need to visit again in the future to eat these and see your shows," she told Amelia.

Valerie's insides did a flip. Her own mother was making plans – loose unspecified plans, but still plans – of frequenting The Rose. She hadn't even dared to think about the future. What would it mean if she made the same intention known? Would Amelia know that it meant more than seeing a colleague? More than seeing a friend? Suddenly, she realized her mom and Amelia were both staring at her.

"What?"

They laughed. "Your mom asked you if you wanted dessert?" Amelia said in a mock whisper.

"No, thanks. Ice cream after margaritas doesn't sit well for me," Valerie said.

"That's a very good point," Elizabeth said, and Amelia nodded in agreement. When the server brought over the bill, Elizabeth insisted on paying, despite Amelia's argument that she could cover it as a gift from a local to a tourist.

After dinner, Amelia said goodbye and Elizabeth pulled her in for a hug and a kiss on the cheek. "You are such a sweet girl," she whispered in her ear, and gave a meaningful squeeze as she said, "I look forward to seeing you again soon." Amelia blushed and looked at Valerie. They enveloped each other with full hugs. Amelia tried not to linger, but being in her arms was like home, like lying in bed under the covers after a long day. She gave Valerie a small, subtle kiss on her collarbone.

Valerie stiffened slightly before giving her a final squeeze and pulling away.

Meanwhile Valerie was stepping away. "I'll see you at rehearsal?" she said, lifting the end like a question.

Amelia nodded and put her professional face back on. "Yes, and it was so nice to meet you, Elizabeth."

Back in her apartment, Amelia wondered at that moment of hesitation Valerie showed in their embrace. Was Valerie upset about the public display of affection? Was it because her mom was there? Amelia's own mother had been kind of distant. Loving, in her own way, but not physically affectionate.

Chapter 21

Valerie snapped a few photos of the pre-set costume pieces left in the dressing room. It had been a longer day than she anticipated. When Amelia had explained to her what a "cue-to-cue" was, it sounded like it would be a breeze. After all, the lighting and sound designers had a dry tech the day before, so all the cues and moments were written, programmed, and set. Things would just need to be adjusted a bit, to make sure that the lighting colors would not clash with the set or costuming.

Except it ended up being a lot more than "simple". Part of it was making the timing right or adjusting the mood of some lighting moments.

Even though the lighting designer had the cues set up, Amelia was the filter for the collective vision. It had to match the image in her head. Too many cooks can spoil the stew, but that's why theatres have directors.

The actors would stand on stage where they would be for each cue. They would start running through lines a moment before in the script so that Jason could call the cue. Which, Valerie found out, was Jason telling the light board and sound board operators when to press their respective 'go' buttons. She thought it would make more sense for Jason to just hit the buttons himself, until she saw that he was manually bringing up and down mic packs to balance the sound.

On stage, the actors did not fully rehearse each scene. They wore their costumes and mostly just waited. Sarah, who had stepped in as Jack's mother, had the book in her hands and one earbud in listening to her music. Amelia was glad she was utilizing her time, but Sarah sang out loud sporadically, lost in her own rehearsal, that it had been disrupting the process even more, and she had to go to the greenroom, with one of the stagehands taking her space onstage whenever necessary.

Valerie looked through some of the b-roll footage she had caught throughout the day. She could tell from looking at this, how Amelia seemed to droop as the day went on. Sure, tensions were rising and patience was dropping as rehearsal stopped as each adjustment had to be made, but had anyone noticed how hard Amelia was working herself? Amelia was the center, not just of this production, but of the entire theatre. She was taking on so much. Hell, the whole reason Valerie was even here was to take one area of the hundreds of tasks off Amelia's shoulders.

Moving toward the office, Valerie found Amelia laying on the chaise lounge with red puffy eyes. "Ames, what's wrong?" Valerie felt fiercely protective.

"It's just overwhelming. So many decisions to make... too much executive function." She choked out a wet laugh. "I think it'll turn out fine. I hope people like it, or at least that the cast and crew won't hate me for being too... particular. And everyone wants me to have all the answers right as they ask the questions. I hate feeling unprepared and I hate feeling like the enemy."

"You're not the enemy, Ames." Valerie took a water bottle out of the mini fridge and handed it to her, holding her hand. "And you are prepared. It's like you told me, things come up. You've been amazing, balancing all these spinning plates."

"You're sweet, V." Amelia sniffed.

"You're not going to be hated by anyone for putting so much care into this show. You're like a coffee filter; everything must go through you. But you do not have to do it alone. You're the captain!"

"A coffee filter and a captain... you really love figurative language, don't you?" Amelia smiled.

"I do," Valerie replied, "and I am not wrong. You have all these ideas that you have to process and go through. So many people coming to you with their interpretations and you have to cater each one to a singular uniformed vision. It's intense. And you are so inspiring. The way you can manage all of this... I wish I could do it."

Amelia let out a small disagreeing huff of air.

"What is it that really has you worried?" Valerie asked. "Is it your uncle?"

She shrugged, "That's part of it, I guess. I just never can be sure what's going to happen. You only get one chance to debut, one chance to make your first step. If I have a sloppy first impression, I'm done for. No one will audition for me again and it would not even matter because there will not be an audience to perform to. This is it, Valerie. This is my one and only first chance." She sagged into Valerie's arms. "If this goes badly, there will not be a 'next time'. I will be done." Amelia started crying, from the stress and the doubt and the fear. Valerie stroked her hair and held her, mummering things like "You're safe," and "Just breathe, Amelia".

It reminded her of the panic attacks she would have when she was younger, after her dad had passed. "Ames?" She mumbled a response into Valerie's collarbone. "Can you tell me five things you can see?"

Amelia sat up, still shaking slightly and looked about the room. "Desk. Chair. Programs. Books. You."

"What about four things you can feel?" Valerie asked.

"The couch. My pants. The air conditioner. Your hands."

Valerie continued the grounding exercise, "Three things you can hear?"

Amelia paused and closed her eyes. "The cast on stage, cars outside, your voice."

"Two things you can smell?" Valerie asked.

"The lavender cotton candle, and your lotion," Amelia said.

"And one thing you can taste?"

Amelia looked up at Valerie, and leaned in for a soft kiss. Valerie felt her pulse quicken.

"You," Amelia said, nestling her head back into Amelia's collarbone.

They stayed there for a while, only breaking their embrace when Amelia got a notification from a group chat for the show that reminded her of the cast party at the Baker's house that night.

"Cast bonding," Amelia explained. "I am exhausted, but I think going would make me feel better."

Valerie pulled her up. "Sounds like exactly what you need."

"Only if you are there with me?" She stated it like a question, and Valerie noticed. She gave her a soft kiss on Amelia's hairline.

"I will gladly go. You deserve to have a good time."

Amelia laughed and Valerie relaxed. *I am falling so hard for you.*

"I think it's really great how much you value cast bonding," Valerie said. "I mean, obviously the cast is all volunteers. I know that you have said that the community theatre scene is like one group even though there are multiple theatres. I don't know, I just think it's cool. You have all these people coming together for a common goal, but you let it be more than just 'nose to the grindstone' for lack of a better phrase. And from what I've seen, you have managed to keep a good balance of fun and work. When it's time for people to work on their scenes, they work. They are diligent and dedicated and they get that from you. I just, really wanted you to know that your hard work is noticed- *you* are noticed."

"Thanks, I really needed to hear that today," Amelia sniffed.

"I know Bert sees you," Valerie smiled.

"Good ol' Bert."

Valerie went over to the fridge to grab a water bottle. "Want some water?"

"Sure."

"Any preference?" Valerie asked. There were a few different brands available.

"Whichever."

"Do you think water has a flavor?" Valerie pondered.

"I don't believe anyone who says they can tell which brand of water they're drinking from the taste," Amelia said. "Like we get it, you are hydrated and want everyone to know it."

Valerie laughed. "Yeah, like, they always say, 'People who drink a lot of water can tell.' Well, I drink a lot of water and I can't tell."

"Unless you do not drink as much water as you think you do," Amelia countered.

"I think it's a conspiracy."

"And yet, you're a Bert Believer."

Valerie laughed, "I'm a diehard Bert Believer, obviously. But seriously, I think one day, some random person decided they wanted to be a water snob. Like maybe they were a former alcoholic, and they could not be a wine snob anymore, so they had to start acting like he knew the different tastes of water."

"Wait. That actually makes a lot of sense. I kind of hate how that makes sense." Amelia shook her head. "I need to turn off the marque, and then we can head out." She opened a door that blended into the wall, Valerie was shocked when Cinderella's Prince jumped out, with Jason behind him. Austin's hair was ruffled, and Jason was pulling his shirt down over a black binder. Jason saw Valerie notice and turned red.

Valerie looked away.

"What the hell?" Amelia's voice was like scalding coffee.

"I should, uh..." Austin said as he grabbed his backpack. "Bye." He walked out.

Amelia turned her attention to Jason.

"I do not want to talk about it," Jason said.

"Well, that's too bad; we are going to talk about it." Amelia turned off the light switch and locked the door.

Valerie felt that the conversation did not need her input. "I will see you at the party."

Amelia nodded; her brow furrowed as she marched towards the stage where Jason had departed to.

Chapter 22

Amelia found Jason crying by the piano. It looked like he had kicked some of the folding chairs over because they were askew on the floor.

"Jason, what is going on?" Amelia said gently.

"Go away."

Amelia sat down on the lip of the stage.

"I don't expect you to understand," Jason said.

"Honey, has he told you that he's queer?" Amelia asked.

Jason's eyes looked like they would skewer her, "I think him sticking his tongue down my throat clarified it. And don't patronize me with the 'honey' bullshit."

Amelia tried another angle. "He dumped you when you came out as trans, Jason."

"He misses me."

"He might miss the old you," Amelia said almost under her breath.

"That's not true!" Jason's face grew red, his arms wrapped around himself.

"Then why was his hand in your binder?"

"Fuck you." Jason's voice was venom.

"Why was he groping your chest?" Amelia pushed back. "I saw, Jason."

"Stop," Jason's voice broke.

"He doesn't see you for the man you are. God, I never should have cast him."

Jason blew his nose. "Do you know how hard it has been for him on stage with those girls? When he wants me? He wants moments in the woods with *me*."

"Then why are you sneaking around to hook up in the marquee closet?"

"He's not ready to come out!"

"Is that it? He told you that?"

"There wasn't a lot of talking, it was mostly... He didn't want people to know." Jason said.

Amelia looked at him with pity. "Jason, you are my best friend. You deserve more than being someone's secret."

"I can't force someone out of the closet! You don't get it, Amelia. I know that you are a strong ally for trans people, and that you understand what it means to be queer, but that's only in the context of loving someone the same gender as you. But you have no concept of what it feels like to be transgender. Me coming out as a man forced Austin to deal with the fact that I am a man. He thought he was straight when he met me. The old me. When I left her behind, it shook him, because of how much he loved me. He still loves me."

"I think you are deluding yourself." Amelia said flatly. "What about his very public showmance with The Baker's Wife?"

"She's just his beard!"

"He's playing you because he's a player and that's what he fucking does. It's like middle school all over again!"

"That was different, we were kids. People grow, people change." Jason countered.

Amelia contemplated that. "Sure, people can change. But not always in the ways we want them to. Austin is straight."

"Who the fuck are you to say what he is? You don't actually know him. Not like I do."

"Okay, you're right. I don't know him very well. But I do know you. And I remember when you were crying in the bathroom because he broke your heart when you were first coming out as trans. He said some really fucked up shit and treated you like a fucking leper." Jason shook his head to block her out or to get her to stop talking but she was on a roll. "You told me at the beginning of all of this that you were done with him. I asked you if it would be a problem or if you would be

139

uncomfortable. I would not have cast him if you asked me not to."

"Maybe it's not about you! He's one of the best people from auditions, and I wasn't going to prevent you having the best in the show." Jason said. "I'm not the one who's uncomfortable."

"Don't make this about me, this is about you and how you need to stay away from him. He's not good for you!"

"You're not the boss of me, Amelia." Jason got up and started to leave.

"I think you're making a mistake trusting him."

"Just give me some space," he said.

Amelia watched Jason storm out of the theatre's emergency exit.

She could not justify recasting Austin so close to opening, not when Jason was adamant that he was okay with him being in the show. Was there a chance that Austin had been honest with Jason? That was unlikely. But there was a chance he was in the closet still. The queer closet, not the marquee closet. She has already seen him storm out.

Amelia thought about calling Valerie, but she had just left and agreed to meet her at the cast party.

The cast party!

For the rest of the night, Amelia decided that she was not going to worry about the show, the drama with Jason and Austin, or her uncle's threats. Instead, she was going to spend the night focused on Valerie.

As soon as she finished one text.

A: *Jason, I am sorry for reacting so harshly. You know I love you, and I just want what's best for you. And you are right, I don't know what it's like to be genderqueer and I hope you know I would never try and assume that I know what it's like. Sexuality and gender are two separate things. I hear you. I*

140

still worry about you, because I love you and I know you'd do the same for me. I promise I will be more compassionate moving forward. Just please be careful. I love you.

A little while later, Jason responded.

J: *I am careful. Can we just drop it for now? I love you, too.*

A: *Like it never happened – for now.*

Amelia put her phone back in her bag and locked up the theatre.

Chapter 23

Valerie had to admit, it felt so good to be a part of something. She looked around at all the different people around her. A month ago, she never would have guessed that she would be in a beach house with a whole cast of fully grown theatre kids. She never would have believed that she'd be here drinking with them, laughing with them, feeling like she was one of them. And she was falling for the ringleader of the whole circus.

Joff, the lighting designer, had brought a concoction of multiple rums called Captain Argyle. Valerie had been nursing her cup for the last hour.

"It is a lot stronger than it seems," Joff had warned her with a goofy grin. "It's gonna be a good time!"

Amelia was having a friendly and very loud debate with Jason about whether Alexander Hamilton or Aaron Burr was the protagonist of a big musical. Valerie had tried to ask Amelia about what happened between her and Jason after they found Jason with Austin in the marquee closet. If she were being honest, it seemed like a big deal, but here at the party, they were acting like nothing had happened. Which did not make sense to Valerie, since she had seen the way Amelia looked ready to breathe fire. But Valerie did notice that Austin was absent from the party. The Baker and The Witch were absent too, but that was because The Witch was really fatigued from the pregnancy hormones.

"From a literary standpoint, Hamilton is his own enemy! He's the protagonist and the antagonist," Jason exclaimed, smacking the table with their hand for emphasis, so it sounded like *an tag o nist.*

Amelia rolled her eyes playfully, "But that's not playable onstage!" She looked over at Valerie. "See? V agrees with me." She grabbed her drink and sat on the couch right next to Valerie… *right next to her.* Their legs were touching, and Amelia wrapped an arm around Valerie's shoulders, leaning her whole body against her. She kept thinking about that kiss. Valerie realized people were staring at her expectantly. "I am sorry what?"

Amelia sighed and sat up straight. She started to talk very fast and used a lot of hand waving in her explanation. "Isn't it the first rule of script analysis that a play needs a playable antagonist? And that the antagonist gets in the way of whatever the protagonist wants? So, if Aaron Burr is constantly faced with Hamilton in his way, would not that make Burr the protagonist?"

Valerie was still thinking about how Amelia's had touched her so casually, like they had touched each other a million times. Her skin was a live wire.

"Do not agree with her, Valerie." Jason pleaded.

Amelia held up her hand with her drink in it as if to silence Jason's protestations, then gave Valerie a pouting face.

How could she say anything other than what Amelia wanted? Valerie shrugged. "Sorry Jason, my hands are tied."

Amelia gave Jason a smug look, who turned away, playfully shaking his head towards the kitchen as if Valerie and Amelia were both insane.

"My right-hand woman," Amelia said, giving Valerie a kiss on the cheek.

"I am left-handed," Valerie said stupidly.

"So, stage right," Amelia said. "Rights and lefts are backwards sometimes. It's hard to explain right now, but trust me, it makes sense."

"I trust you," Valerie said, surprised by how true it was. This was a level of trust that she had never felt with a romantic partner.

Not that they were romantic partners. *Get a grip,* Valerie commanded herself. She put her drink down even though she had only had a few sips. She did not want to say the wrong thing. *A few moments does not make you a couple,* Valerie

143

thought. She looked back at Amelia, knowing that she would gladly spend all her time in Amelia's presence.

Amelia did not react to Valerie's internal monologue; she was busy looking around at the party. She felt detached from it all, as if this couch which held Valerie and herself was an island all its own. Valerie felt stiff beside her, and Amelia wished she would relax, wished that they could sit on a couch together comfortably, wished they could cuddle and fall asleep here, wished they were alone.

"I think I'm tired," Amelia said, barely more than a whisper but it was enough.

Valerie took her hand, "Do you need a ride? You shouldn't drive."

That was sweet, Amelia thought. They stood up and Valerie took note of how Amelia seemed to wobble.

"Hey, Jason? I am going to take Ames home," she said. Amelia was too busy trying not to get too disoriented. She really regretted those shots with Jason. And the three cups of Captain Argyle. That stuff really was dangerous. She'd need to get the recipe from Joff. And also make sure he always brought it to cast parties in the future.

Valerie helped Amelia into her car and started driving. Jason had put the address in Valerie's phone before they left, and Amelia felt the sweet pull of sleep tugging at her.

"What it is about being in cars at nighttime?" Amelia asked.

"What do you mean?"

"It's like, the most peaceful and calming ambient noise. And the cold air conditioner, and the warmth of the alcohol. Being a passenger in cars at nighttime is the best kind of tired."

"Well, as long as you are the passenger and not the driver when you drink," Valerie said.

"No drinking and driving," Amelia nodded. "Passenger is way better. Cozy. Safe." Amelia paused for a moment, "I'm sorry," she said.

"It's alright, Ames." Valerie said. "You work hard, you are allowed to have a good time."

Amelia looked at Valerie. She had both hands on the steering wheel in the DMV approved 10 and 2 positions. She was so focused. The air conditioner was on high, and Amelia shivered.

Valerie noticed that too. "I'll turn it down a bit," she said, turning the fan intensity from four to one.

"Thanks," Amelia said. The car was soothing and quiet. She watched Valerie's features come in and out of focus as the car drove along Pacific Coast Highway, the streetlights illuminating her in cycles like the moon. Sometimes, for brief seconds, the light would shine just right so Amelia could see the aquamarine hair dye peeping through.

"Can I tell you something?"

Valerie's lips twitched into a small smile. "Sure."

Amelia hesitated, "You are ridiculously pretty."

Valerie laughed and it was beautiful. "Well, thank you," she said, "I will always accept compliments."

"No really. You're so pretty, you're like… art." Amelia said.

When they arrived at Amelia's apartment, Valerie helped her up the stairs. The apartment was on the second floor. The door opened to a rectangular living room conjunct with a kitchen, the two were separated by a peninsula island that had the stove and oven on it. The right side of the living room branched off into a small hallway. If you could call it a hallway, it was more of an alcove with three doors. The first on the left was ajar and led to a bathroom, the middle door was closed, and the third door was wide open showing a bedroom. There was a full-size bed with white bedding and a blue nightstand that had been hand painted with flowers growing up the legs. Valerie followed Amelia into this room. There was also a desk covered in books on directing and the art of theatre. Next to it on the floor were two small plastic bins filled with plays. There was no dresser, but there was a small walk-in closet.

Amelia flopped down on the bed. "Don't leave me," she asked. Valerie went into the closet and picked out some pajamas for her to change into.

"Go take a shower," she instructed. "I am going to make you something to eat."

Amelia did what she was told. She intentionally left the door to the bathroom unlocked. Then she took her time in the shower. Partially because it felt amazing and partially hoping that Valerie would join her.

But of course, she didn't. And after using too much water, she decided to get dressed. She was a little worried that Valerie had left, until she opened the door and smelt warm pancakes.

"Are you an angel?" she asked, turning into the kitchen. Valerie had lit some candles and made pancakes for her.

Valerie laughed again. Amelia felt like she was winning each time she heard that beautiful laugh.

"I lit some candles because your lights are really bright, and I don't want you to get a headache."

"A little late for that one," Amelia said, squinting her eyes and rubbing the middle of her forehead.

Valerie hopped up and grabbed her bag, taking out a small bottle of Advil. "An appetizer then, here. And I want you to drink as much of this water as you can."

They ate their pancakes in a comfortable quiet- except for the hum of the refrigerator and the sound of conversations on the neighbor's balcony. When Amelia was done eating, Valerie picked up the dishes, rinsed them, and put them in the dishwasher.

"You drank all the water, good job." Valerie said as she refilled the glass. "It's time for you to lay down and get some rest."

"Will you stay?" Amelia asked. She knew it might make her seem desperate, but she was past that. She just wanted to hold this beautiful woman close as she drifted off.

Valerie didn't respond, but pulled back the sheets to the bed and tucked Amelia in.

It felt so nice to be tucked in, to be cared for. Sleep was already pulling her eyes closed and her body was sinking into her bed. "Stay. Please," she managed to say.

"Okay," Valerie said. She crawled into bed, not quite touching.

Valerie thought she was already asleep and did not know that Amelia felt it when she pushed her hair behind her ear and placed a small kiss on Amelia's temple before sliding out of the bed, back into the kitchen.

Chapter 24

In the morning, Amelia woke up feeling tired, but not as nearly as hungover as she thought she would.

When she went out to go to the bathroom, she saw that Valerie had slept on the sofa. Not being the chef that Valerie was, she ordered some coffee and scones for them on her phone to be delivered. She wanted to replay last night, to experience it all over again, but sober. Maybe extend the night and stay up with Valerie for hours.

"Good morning," Valerie mumbled, pulling Amelia out of her thoughts.

"Hi, good morning." Amelia replied. "You could've slept in the bed; that couch could not have been comfortable."

Valerie sat up and stretched. "It was alright. And Amelia, you were plastered last night. I wasn't just going to invite myself into your bed."

Amelia was unsure of how to reply to that. Thankfully, she didn't have to. Her phone chimed to let her know that the coffee and scones she had ordered had arrived. She went to the door and collected their breakfast from her porch and handed a cup to Valerie.

"This is a thank you," she sat down next to Valerie on the couch.

"For what?" Valerie asked.

"For last night. Bringing me home, making pancakes, all of it. It was sweet. I probably could have slept at Jason's. But it was really nice to wake up in my own bed, clean from the shower. And the pancakes were great. I think they helped a lot too." Amelia said.

"I wanted to make sure you were okay, and I wanted to take care of you," Valerie said, her thumb running along the edge of the cardboard holder around the to-go coffee cup. "I wasn't sure what was going on with you and Jason after the thing yesterday with Austin, and I knew that if I went back to the hotel, I would have been up all night worrying about you."

Amelia felt fluttering in her chest. "You would have worried?"

"Yes." Valerie looked right at her.

The moment slowed down. Once again, like in the costume loft that feeling of tension, the inhale before the dive, like even time was holding its breath.

"V?" Amelia asked, her eyes fixed on Valerie's lips.

"Yes." Valerie said again.

And then their lips collided. The kiss grew from soft to fueled by all the longing from the last few weeks. It was everything, every moment since that first kiss in front of the theatre.

It was an answer. It was a question.

It was a kiss to fan a spark to flame.

It was a kiss to tell stories about.

It was everything.

The kiss was hungry, their tongues and hands exploring.

"I want you," Amelia said. Valerie almost stopped. There was so much risk, the risk of everything crashing and burning. The risk that she would get invested and Amelia would get tired of her. But why should the moment suffer because of fear for the future?

"I do too," she decided.

Valerie pulled Amelia down on the couch until she was straddling her, Valerie turned her face up to keep kissing her while their arms wrapped around each other.

Valerie found the bottom of Amelia's pajama top and grazed a hand along her bare back. Amelia felt tingles and pins and needles throughout her spine. The ache of longing pooling at her core.

"Bed?" Amelia offered.

Valerie nodded. Amelia gave another passionate kiss, biting Valerie's lip slightly as she pulled away. Valerie moaned and followed her to the bedroom.

"I'm clean," Valerie said.

"Me too," Amelia said. "I have some protection if you want though."

"I don't need it," Valerie said. Then she grabbed Amelia by the hips and pulled her in. With one hand, she brushed Amelia's hair out of the way and started kissing her neck. She dragged her tongue along the length of Amelia's neck, then started sucking along her collarbone.

Amelia's eyes fluttered closed, and she reached up slowly. She felt Valerie's rib cage and slid her hand up to tenderly touch her breast. Her hand was too small to hold it all. She lifted it gently and ran her thumb over the nipple softly until she felt it harden.

Valerie pulled away to take her shirt off. Amelia did the same and sat down on the bed. Valerie knelt in front of her, softly kissing her way from Amelia's collarbone to a spot above her left hip. She hooked a finger into the waistband of Amelia's shorts. One finger at a time, she hooked her hand into the waistband and then flattened her palm against Amelia's perfect ass. She slid her hand down on one side, bringing the shorts and underwear down while her other hand pulled the other side down.

"Valerie, you don't have to," Amelia started.

"Shh." Valerie kissed the inner side of Amelia's knee and started to make her way up her thighs. Amelia could feel Valerie's wicked smile. "If you want me to stop, say 'peaches'. Okay?"

"Okay," Amelia said.

"Now let me worship you like the goddess you are."

Amelia laid back and looked at her ceiling. As Valerie got closer, she wondered if she should have shaved; would Valerie think body hair was gross? But then, she was there. Her tongue parting her wet slit in long wide strokes. She trembled and tried unsuccessfully to stifle a moan.

"Don't quiet yourself," Valerie ordered. "Let me hear you."

Then she started to use her mouth faster. Then she started using her hand to circle around her clit.

"Can I go inside?" Valerie asked.

"Yes," Amelia whimpered.

Valerie brought her mouth back down onto her clit, she sucked as she entered one finger into Amelia's vagina. Then two. She kept thrusting and licking until Amelia screamed and arched her back as orgasm took her over.

She was panting and Valerie left a trail of wet kisses along Amelia's torso as she came up onto the bed. She brushed Amelia's hair out of her eyes and kissed her forehead.

"You are so fucking beautiful," Valerie said.

They held each other on the bed, Amelia the small spoon.

"I know it's probably too soon," Amelia said.

"Amelia," Valerie interrupted.

"No please, let me say this." She took a deep breath. "You do not need to say it back. And there's no expectation. I know you probably don't fall as easily as I do – but I do. I see whole constellations in your eyes, and I think I am falling for you. And it feels like falling sometimes, like right now. It's exhilarating and terrifying. And sometimes it feels like floating; you calm me, you understand what I need. I know that you just got out of a relationship before coming here. I know that you have so many reasons to be hesitant to start anything with me. Including the fact that you live so far away, but I think, if you wanted to, we could make this work. I think, maybe, we should just see where it goes. We both deserve the chance to try."

Valerie had been silent throughout Amelia's speech. She had listened and pondered. There were so many things to say. Where to start?

"I care about you, Ames." She said, she entwined their fingers, so their palms were against each other. "You mean so much to me, it's scary. The logistics aren't as daunting as the thought of leaving after this show and never seeing you again."

The truth was that Valerie was so scared of being hurt again. Things with Stacy were rocky for a long time, and they should have ended it sooner. Those weeks, months, of drifting apart; that void of being tethered to someone but not being able to feel them on the other side of the connection. It was an isolating kind of loneliness. She wanted to make things work, but at the end of the day, Stacy still cheated on her. Valerie could not shake the fear of not being good enough. How long would it be before Amelia decided that she was bored? Would the distance make their hearts grow fonder? Or would it be like pouring gasoline in a garden, killing the seeds that had not even gotten a chance to sprout or bloom?

There were too many unknowns. Too many risks. And she wanted to cherish this time with Amelia, because realistically, this was the only time they could be sure of. When she went back to Washington, she was sure that Amelia would move on with someone else. Valerie could not bear the thought of being betrayed again. So, she concluded that if she never offered Amelia forever, then forever could never be cut short.

Amelia noticed that Valerie hadn't said the L word. Neither had she, really. But there was a part of her that was waiting for a green light from Valerie. Amelia had been single longer than her, so Valerie was the one who had to decide if it was a good time. No one wants to develop feelings for someone just to find out later that they were being used as a distraction or rebound. If this was just a rebound, would that change things? Amelia was not sure. She debated it internally. She wanted to ask outright, but that felt wrong somehow. She needed tact. Plus, her career might not be what Valerie wanted in a partner. If Valerie even wanted a partner.

"My longest relationship was two years," Amelia said. "We fell hard and fast and then she left. She decided she wanted someone who was not a theatre person. I was busy with rehearsals, and it was a lot of time commitment. She didn't like it. So, when we were together, I became a level 5 clinger. And she hated that too. At the end of the day, she wanted me available to her when it was convenient for her. And she was, honestly, really back and forth. I tried everything to change for her. Which is, you know, not great. It took me a long time to find myself again at the end of that relationship. I did not even realize how much I had changed for her." *There, that's one insecurity out in the open.*

"That's awful. I am so sorry. No one deserves to feel like that."

"I don't want to make you feel trapped," Amelia said.

"And I don't want you to feel abandoned," Valerie said. Somehow, Amelia felt like that answered more than one question, while still not answering anything. Valerie did not know how much to say. She did not want Amelia to feel like a part time temporary quick romance, but what else could she offer? They were two ships heading for separate seas.

"We should get ready," Amelia said.

"I left all my stuff at the hotel," Valerie groaned.

"Let me get my things, we can get ready there."

"And we have plenty of time, if you want a round two," Valerie said, that wicked smile playing on the corners of her lips again. Amelia felt weak in the knees already, longing for Valerie all over again.

Chapter 25

Back at the hotel, Valerie and Amelia could barely close the door before they were all over each other again. The added pressure of the time ticking to opening night, the anxiety of the night itself and what success or failure would mean for each of them individually, and the knowledge that they were on the cusp of a chasm of feelings all came together like lightning on a dry tree. The flames did not need to be fanned.

"Set an alarm," Valerie said as she kicked off her shoes. Amelia flopped on the bed on her stomach. She set an alarm on her phone and tossed it onto the nightstand. Valerie was already above her, brushing her loose red hair to one side to kiss her neck.

"Be careful not to leave any marks," she said.

"At least none that anyone will see." Valerie flipped Amelia over then. One hand went up Amelia's shirt. "No bra, easier access."

"Well," Amelia tried to sound lighthearted, but Valerie had lowered her mouth onto her breast, "time restrictions." She shivered as Valerie sucked on her, bit her, kissed her. Amelia pulled Valerie's face up to hers and kissed her hard. Their tongues traced each other's lips, exploring tentatively. Amelia bit softly and pulled Valerie's bottom lip.

Valerie's groan was primal. She lifted Amelia's shirt up to remove it. The bottom of the shirt went over her head and Valerie left it on her, upside down, the neck of the shirt on the bridge of Amelia's nose, her arms restrained ever so slightly above her head.

"Fuck, Ames," Valerie said, removing her own shirt and bra.

"I want to feel you," Amelia said, removing the shirt fully, and sitting up to kneel on the bed facing Valerie.

Chest to chest, they held each other. Soon, their bottoms were gone, they were both fully naked, fully together in that moment. Amelia pulled Valerie closer, until they were each half sitting on one of the other's thighs.

They kissed as their bodies started grinding. Their hands exploring as they consumed one another. Valerie had never felt pleasure like this before. "Sex with you is going to ruin me," she said.

"Good," Amelia replied.

Neither of them wanted to admit they felt the pressure of the clock, the limited number of days they had together. Each waited for the other to bring up "after". What were they going to be to each other after final bows for *Into the Woods*?

Too soon, the alarm went off that it was time to get ready.

Valerie moaned but kissed Amelia softly. "Ready to take a shower?" She led her into the bathroom, not bothering to close the door.

In the shower, Amelia washed Valerie's body. The hotel had provided an exfoliating citrus scented soap bar. She lathered it on each soft curve. Valerie had never had someone do that for her before. It was intimate. All the while, Amelia saying "You're beautiful," and leaving little kisses above her hip bone, behind her knee, on her shoulder, and at the spot where her breasts connected to the center of her chest.

As Valerie got dressed, Amelia put on lotion. That honey and copal scent wafted through the air. "This lotion is addicting as hell; did you know that?" Valerie asked, kissing her nose.

"I'm glad you like it. It's my favorite."

"Mine too, now."

Valerie put on her Docs, mid length skirt - black and crowded with white pebble stone design, and a flowy black crop top.

They went to the theatre where Amelia had left her outfit for the night. Amelia looked amazing, of course. By the

155

time zipped up her dress, Valerie was trying hard not to look like she was on the verge of drooling, which of course she was. Amelia's copper hair was up in two braids that crossed from ear to ear along the back of her neck, with the blonde money pieces in the front left out in loose curls. Her one shoulder wrap dress was deep purple and clung deliciously along her curves, and there was the broach, about two inches long, in the shape of a golden rose that she was pinning along the shoulder strap. She was wearing fake pearl earrings and a simple golden chain necklace.

"I guess this is as good as it's going to get," she said, looking over her ensemble in the mirror.

"I don't think there's a higher standard to meet, you're already perfect." Valerie said.

Amelia blushed and grabbed her phone. "Oh my gosh, it's almost six! I need to make sure all the dressing rooms are ready."

"They're ready, I just checked."

"The booth?"

"We set it yesterday."

"What about the house? If the seating is messy or anything- "

"Then you can have Jason handle it; you are not going to be mopping up anything in that dress. You put in all the hard work already. Tonight is your night to enjoy the rewards of your labors."

Amelia snickered. "Of my labors? Who talks like that?"

"I got you to smile," Valerie said. Amelia used both hands to hold hers, looking intently at the lines on Valerie's palm. "I wish I knew how to read palms," she said, "I tried learning when I was a little kid. See this one is your lifeline, and this one is your head line, and your heart line…" she trailed off, tracing the lines on Valerie's palm with care, like they were ancient hieroglyphics or precious words in a love letter.

"What can you see?"

Amelia smiled that soft smile, "If I could see anything, I wouldn't be so nervous right now," she said, looking up at Valerie. Valerie wanted to ask why she was nervous, hoping it was the same reason as her… but before she had the chance, Amelia took one hand around the back of Valerie's neck, and pulled her in for a kiss.

The effect was immediate. Valerie felt that rush of adrenaline throughout her body, she fought the urge to grab Amelia and run her fingers through her beautiful copper hair… with the hand that wasn't being held still, she cupped Amelia's face. Amelia pulled away slightly, resting her forehead on Valerie's cheek.

After a moment, Valerie said, "I am nervous too, and if you do that again, we might end up missing the play."

There was a pang in Valerie's chest and Amelia started welcoming patrons into the lobby. She was so in her element, and Valerie could tell she was nervous. The anxiety of opening night was one thing, but with the show opening, that meant that she was running out of time, and it was hard to forget.

Valerie took a quick tour of the house and made sure all the seats were clear of trash, and that the curtain was closed.

"You got some pre-show jitters?" Jason asked.

"Yeah, I guess so," Valerie said. "People are starting to arrive."

"Already? That's good! Can you do me a favor and keep an eye on our girl?"

Valerie nodded and headed back out to the lobby. Coming around the bend, she saw Amelia standing by the front doors handing out programs to an elderly couple walking in. She started to walk toward Amelia, but was stopped when someone grabbed her by the wrist.

"I have been looking everywhere for you."

Valerie stopped in her tracks and looked at the person holding her wrist.

"Stacy?"

157

Chapter 26

Stacy was undoubtedly there in front of her, wearing a two-piece shimmering emerald gown, the top a cropped stringy thing that exposed her breasts and midriff, the shirt was floor-length with a slit that came all the way up to her right hip.

"I missed you! This theatre is so cute, very... what's the right word? Quaint? Vintage?" Stacy said. "Although sometimes I think people just say something is vintage when they really mean that they can't afford to upgrade a place."

leaning in to kiss Valerie. For her part, Valerie was able to turn her head at the last moment to orchestrate a kiss on the cheek instead. Valerie looked over at Amelia, who was looking at her, shock slapped on her face.

"What are you doing here?" was all Valerie managed to say.

"Val," Stacy stretched out the nickname in two syllables like a worn-out welcome, "I am here to be a supportive girlfriend, obviously. Like we talked about."

Jason was opening another bottle of champagne at the bar.

"Oh, I'd love a glass," Stacy placed a hand on Valerie's, bringing it behind her, around her waist.

"I'll get you one." Valerie tried to walk away from Stacy, but her ex followed her over to the bar. She knew that if she did not get rid of Stacy soon, things with Amelia could get really complicated. And she did not, under any circumstances, want to have Stacy of all people get between her and Amelia. Not now. Not that they were finally... well, they hadn't gotten around to labels yet. But that was the whole point, as far as Valerie was concerned.

"A champagne, please, Jason?"

Jason looked at Stacy, who was leaning territorially all over Valerie and raised an eyebrow.

"How's everything going over here?" Amelia asked as she went behind the bar where Jason was.

"Oh, are you the client?" Stacy asked in a tone that implied she already knew who Amelia was and how Valerie felt about her. Stacy looked Amelia up and down, as if measuring an unworthy opponent. "This little set up is so adorable. Honestly, Val is such a sweetheart for taking on your case. This kind of fieldwork is typically beneath her. I just love how charitable she is."

"Stacy, that's enough." Valerie said, trying once again to create physical distance, but Stacy's arm coiled around hers like a snake around a mouse.

"Yes, it is." Amelia said, with that inner fire Valerie loved so much. With the air of perfect professionalism, Amelia dismissed them with an "enjoy the show!" and her eyes welcomed a different patron to the bar counter to place an order.

"Stacy, what the hell?" Valerie said.

Stacy dropped her clingy act. "I told you, I am here to support you. Val, I tried calling."

"I blocked you."

Stacy's eyes narrowed. She shook her shoulders slightly and stood up straighter. "I want to make this work, Val. That other girl was a mistake, she was nothing to me. It was just sex, just for fun. Practically a toy. There was no emotion there. I only love you."

"You only love yourself. You cheated on me. And honestly, hearing you describe your affair like an inanimate object is disgusting. She's a *person*, Stacy. *I* am a person."

"It wasn't like that," Stacy huffed. "God it wasn't an *affair*, it was a *mistake.*"

"It's crazy how you don't understand that mistakes aren't repetitive."

"Oh, so now you're calling me crazy?" Stacy bellowed.

159

Valerie noticed a few of the patrons were starting to look their way. "Let's go outside."

Out in the cool air, Valerie could smell the sea and feel the mist in the air coming off that marina layer. "Already wanting to be alone with me?" Stacy cooed, interrupting the beauty of the night. The light of the marquee was lighting up the street and reflecting off the condensation on the cars and the ground. Stacy snaked her hands around Valerie. "Let's get out of here. You have a hotel room, right?"

Valerie grabbed her wrists and pushed her away. "Stop, people are starting to stare."

"So?" Stacy pouted.

"So, I'm working, and I don't want to distract anyone from the show."

"Why? Because of the skanky redhead?"

"Stacy, fucking stop. Don't talk about her like that." Valerie was trying to keep her cool, but Stacy knew which buttons to push. "Because it's my job to do everything I can to make this night successful. Because I do not want people staring at us and I do not want you to make a scene. Because I do not want to spend another minute fighting with my ex-girlfriend who showed up out of the blue. Because of a million reasons and yes, most of them are because of Amelia which honestly is none of your business."

"I tried calling, I told you... Val, I have to talk to you," Stacy pleaded.

"What is so urgent?"

"Val, I know I messed up, and I want to make it right, but I don't know how. I want to fix this, you and me. We can get through this."

Valerie sighed and put her hands in her pockets. She glanced inside and saw that the lobby was emptying out as patrons made their way to their seats. The show would be starting soon and she did not want to miss Amelia's welcome speech.

"I want you to marry me." Stacy said.

"What?" That had gotten Valerie's attention.

160

"No one else loves me the way you do. You take care of me when I am sick, you always tell me I am beautiful. I did not realize how much you loved me until you were gone, until I had to wake up alone. You used to make me coffee in the morning. You used to clean the kitchen. You were there for me."

"It sounds like you want a maid, not a girlfriend," Valerie muttered.

"Oh my god, I am not saying this right. I just… I was in a dark headspace. I know, I know I am not good enough for you. I do this, Val, you know me, I self-sabotage."

"I can't trust you, Stacy! Don't you get that? I cannot even look at you right now. And this isn't just because you cheated on me. You know as well as I do that our relationship had been on the rocks for a while. We should have ended things months ago!"

"That's not true," Stacy said softly, looking at the floor. Valerie could tell that Stacy was trying not to cry.

"Isn't it? Can you look me in the eyes and tell me the last time we were happy together? The last time we even spent time together. Not me serving you, not sex, just having a good time together."

For a few moments, she was quiet. Her eyes scanning back and forth in the distance, looking for an answer. Valerie waited.

"What do you want me to say?" Stacy said.

"Nothing. There is nothing to say. I just want you to go."

They looked at each other for a moment. Valerie felt the echo of heartbreak, like poking a bruise that was almost healed. Without warning, Stacy went in for a kiss. No build, no preamble. Just a lot of tongue and grabbing handfuls of Valerie's short hair. Valerie felt nothing, not a spark, not even a glow of an ember. The kiss was just very wet and cold in the sea air. If there were a word for the emotion, she could not find it. Something akin to a numb disappointment. She put her hands on Stacy's shoulders and pushed her away, finally creating enough physical distance to be clear that there was no longer any intimate connection between them. She glimpsed Amelia in the lobby walking toward them.

"Stacy, listen to me. We are broken up," Valerie said gently, "I hope the best for you, but I've moved on."

Amelia opened the door then. Stacy turned and when she saw Amelia, her face and voice went feral.

"You are a fucking cunt," she said, striding into the lobby, pure rage and disappointment and anger. She grabbed a glass of wine out of someone's hand.

Everything was in slow motion. Stacy was pouring the glass of red wine into a box of programs. The small crowd watched in shock, mouths slightly ajar mid-gasp. Amelia's color was draining from her face as she gripped Jason's arm. Jason meanwhile was yelling at Conner to do his job as security. All the while, the millisecond dragged on, and Valerie stood there dumbfounded as to what to do. The programs were ruined but stopping the continuation of the pour was the only action that came to mind.

Valerie kicked the box of programs to the side and tried to grab the wine glass out of Stacy's hand. Stacy smashed it on the floor before she could. Paige's husband, who volunteered to help as security, came up and ushered Stacy back outside. "Ma'am, I will call the police," he warned. Stacy looked around at the people in the lobby. At this point, several people had their phones out recording or live streaming.

"Valerie, you are a bitch," Stacy called out, tears of anger starting to stream down her face. "You're an awful fucking person and I never want to see you again." Then she turned her attention to the crowd. "Don't even bother staying for the show! They'll probably scam you out of your money and your girlfriends!" She yelled as she was led out of the building. "They're probably screwing each other! Fucking cheating bitch!" Stacy hurled each last word as a barb into the lobby.

The door closed and the silence was deafening. Valerie felt like throwing up, so many people were looking at her with wide eyes.

"My apologies, everyone," Amelia said once Stacy was out of sight. "Enjoy your evening, the show will be starting soon." Jason turned up the pre-show music in the house so it could be heard in the lobby. The crowd slowly returned to their chatter, and crew members finished cleaning up the glass before Valerie finished giving a new glass of wine to the man whose had been snatched and shattered.

"So. That was the ex-girlfriend." Amelia said, in the office trying to save any dry programs at the bottom of the box.

"Yep." Valerie said.

"And she was here to…?"

"Propose. Kind of, I think she was just realizing that she messed up and thought I would fold and get back together with her." Valerie really was not looking forward to the many possible states of disaster her apartment would be in when she got back.

Amelia was silent.

"I am sorry she targeted you like that. Are you ok?"

"I am fine; I've been called worse by worse and I have another box of programs," Amelia said a little stiffly.

"That's all you were worried about. The programs?" Valerie tried to joke. Amelia was quiet. "Don't they call that a pre-show?" she tried again. Still, Amelia did not respond. Her silence was making things worse.

"Ames, please," Valerie took her hands. "Talk to me."

Amelia had the beginnings of tears welling up in her eyes. When she spoke, her voice was soft, "I know you say you are over her, but is there anything else I need to know? I don't like secrets. Especially not visits from unhinged exes."

"Nothing to hide here. And I do not have any crazy ex-girlfriend encounters planned for the next month, at least." Valerie smiled.

"I just," Amelia took a deep breath, "You are so fun to be around. You're considerate and caring. You encourage me. I love spending time with you, watching shows and listening to music. Driving around sounds so boring but you make it fun. You make me so happy and I… these last few weeks have been wild. Pure magic. I do not know if the stars have aligned or what is going on, but I swear that these last few weeks…"

Valerie's heart squeezed.

"Valerie, I have fallen head over heels for you. I finally feel like I have two legs to stand on after years of crawling. You're the stability I have always longed for. I love you."

Amelia looked at her with those wide eyes. She was speechless.

Before she could answer, Jason opened the door.

"Showtime, baby!" he cheered, and then went back out.

Amelia dabbed the corners of her eyes. "I need to go start the show." She ran her hands down her hips nervously and Valerie saw the tightness in her shoulders creep back.

"I saved you a seat, right next to me in the booth."

"Best seat in the house," Amelia said. Valerie gave her a soft and tender kiss on her forehead and breathed in the sweet citrus scent of her lotion.

Valerie's phone rang. It was from Matt. "I need to take this. One second," Valerie said.

"I am going to check on the cast." Amelia said, walking out of the office. "See you soon."

Chapter 27

Valerie answered the phone on the third ring. "Hey, how is the business going?" Matt's voice was distracted even over the phone. Well, to be fair he always sounded distracted when talking to Valerie, but this time *he* had called her.

"Great! I think we are almost sold out!" Valerie said, trying to get back onto the high of opening night that was electrifying the air; trying to hide the heaviness that had taken over the evening.

"You mean *they* are almost sold out," he said. "We are not part of the theatre; it is their business. Not ours. Is the client there?"

"Amelia is checking on the cast right now," she said, "did you need to talk to her?" Valerie could not imagine what Matt would need to say that was so urgent.

"That's not what I have here in the folder," Matt said. Valerie could hear the rustle of paperwork. "Mr. Packet, I believe?"

"That's the business owner's uncle," Valerie clarified, "I saw him come in earlier. He's sitting in the audience; did you need to talk to him?" Valerie liked that idea even less than Matt talking to Amelia right now. She could only imagine how he would describe the Stacy incident to her boss.

"No, no. We just got off the phone." *Shit, already?* "He was telling me that there was a scandal outside which seems to have involved you."

Valerie let the air out of her lungs. "Yes. I handled it though," she began to explain.

"Even so, I think it's best for all parties involved that you come on back to base." Matt railroaded.

165

Valerie's mouth dropped, "But I have two more weeks." She sounded like a child complaining that it was bedtime, even to her own ears. She had been counting on that time, those weeks after opening where there would be evenings without rehearsals. Weeknights where she could spend time with Amelia. Weekdays to talk and define their intentions. Amelia had told her that she loved her, but where did they go from here? A declaration of love was not enough to build a relationship that could survive long distance.

Matt did not even respond to her outburst. He just told her to head home first thing in the morning so she could come into work on Monday. "We need to discuss this in the office," and then he hung up.

Valerie stood there as her heart sank to her abdomen. To get home before work Monday, and to have time to sleep, she'd have to leave in the morning. She debated on how and when to tell Amelia. She could not tell her before starting the show, Amelia was already under so much pressure with Uncle Glen and the general opening night anxieties. Stacy's surprise visit also shook her up, and that was undoubtedly Valerie's fault. How could she drop another bomb on her?

But should she really put it off until the morning she was leaving?

Those appeared to be the only two options.

And Valerie decided that they were both horrible. "Bert, what do I do?" The ghost did not respond.

She heard the five-tone chime of the xylophone by concession, *doo da ding da doo.* This meant that concessions were closed until intermission. She shoved her phone in her pocket and hurried towards the booth.

166

The audience was not sold out, but at eighty five percent capacity. *Not bad for an opening night*, Valerie thought.

"At least the audience has a good energy," Jason said as Valerie entered the booth.

"Energy?" Valerie replied, distracted.

"Yeah, I think these are friends and family and other theatre people from the community. It's good for a reactive crowd."

Valerie shrugged, "Like engagement online?"

Jason laughed. "Yes, I guess so. Anyway, we have you to thank for this," Jason said. "I mean, you got the word out and now we have a great turn out for opening night." He gave her a hug and went down to the stage.

Valerie smiled, but her face felt like a mask, even to herself. Valerie watched as Amelia moved like water through the crowd to the stage. Amelia was like bubbles in champagne, she was rushing, floating up; absolutely on top of the world.

"Hello, everyone! Good evening!" The light board operator lowered the house lights, and Amelia dazzled under the spotlight. "Welcome to The Rose Theatre for our debut! We have a great show for you tonight. I recognize some of you theatregoers, and I see some new faces as well. We are so glad you are here."

Valerie swore she saw Amelia look right at her when she said that last part, as if Valerie was the only audience member in the world.

"We are still living in a pandemic, so I want to encourage you to wear your masks. In the event of an emergency, the exits from the theatre are on either the left or right side of the audience. We will be continuing concessions at intermission, but I'd like to remind you to pick up your trash. There are trash cans at the bottom of both ramps, and in the lobby. Please silence your phones or smart watches and refrain from any flash photography or recording of the show as that is distracting to both the cast and your fellow audience members. My stage manager is back there in the booth and can see if you have your phone out, so don't think you can hide!" The audience laughed at that. "And finally, enjoy *Into the Woods*!"

167

Amelia came up to the booth as Jason spoke into the microphone, reminding the audience to refrain from photography and turn their phones off. The show went smoothly, as far as Valerie could tell. She was, admittedly, not paying attention. Amelia's hand was on her thigh, just above the knee. Valerie did not know how to tell her that she had to leave tomorrow.

She could not tell her tonight; it was Amelia's night. She did not want to detract from that. So instead, Valerie sat there; next to the woman she was falling in love with. She hadn't even told her. Maybe she shouldn't.

Amelia had so much going on, that Valerie wasn't sure what to do. She could tell Amelia the whole truth- that she had to go back to Washington, and they could try long distance.

Or she could say nothing and disappear. Maybe leave a note or something? What would be the best way? Her heart ached to think of leaving Amelia. But the last thing Ames needed was a long-distance girlfriend to keep up with on top of all the other things she was responsible for.

Meanwhile, Amelia was absorbing the audience's reactions to the show. Each laugh felt like a victory. By intermission, she was ecstatic. She was so overwhelmed with joy that she could hardly tell Valerie seemed elsewhere. She wanted to ask, but there were only a few minutes until Act II and she wanted to check in with the cast.

"I'm going backstage, want to come with me?"

"Sure."

Amelia smiled and kissed her on the cheek before nearly running down to the stage.

"Great show, everyone!" Amelia beamed. The whole cast was floating on air from the rush of Act I. "You all have great energy, and that is a really responsive crowd. So please remember to articulate and do not upstage yourselves. I am proud of you all, break legs for Act II!"

Act two went by quickly. When the show ended there was a standing ovation and Valerie caught it all on video. Amelia was exhilarated. There was no way for Valerie to bring her down. In the back of her mind, she was dreading the long drive back to Washington.

"We should celebrate!" Amelia said.

"Hell yes, drinks at Grill and Vine?" Jason said.

Valerie nodded and smiled and went along with the commotion. The night passed in a blur, as much as she tried to savor each moment, the time was slipping by faster than she could process. The grief of knowing that her time here was ending was drowning out everything else.

"Are you okay?" Amelia asked. "You have been really quiet."

"I'm just tired," Valerie said. Her heart sinking. A bar full of celebratory theatre kids was not the time to tell a lover/almost girlfriend that time is up.

"We could leave?" She leaned in close. "We could have some peaches," she whispered and kissed under her ear.

Valerie's heart felt punctured.

"Amelia! We are ordering funnel cake!" Jason called from the other end of the table.

"You should stay," Valerie said. "Celebrate with your cast. Enjoy yourself."

"Are you sure?" Amelia said. Valerie could see that she was torn, wanting to be with the cast, wanting to be with her. She could never make her choose.

"Yeah," she said, more confident than she felt, "I really am exhausted, and I need to rest." *That's not a lie, at least. I have hours of driving to do tomorrow; I need to start early to try and avoid the worst of the traffic.*

Amelia cupped Valerie's face and kissed her cheekbone softly. "Get some rest then, darling."

Walking out of that bar was the hardest thing Valerie had ever done. She focused on keeping her back straight, intentionally placing one foot in front of the other. She had to make sure that if Amelia was watching her walk away, she would not notice how badly she wished she could stay.

Chapter 28

The day before had been a dream. Even sleeping, Amelia's subconscious could not conjure anything to compare. From the morning (and afternoon) with Valerie, to the stellar opening night, the whole day had been immaculate. Except for the run-in with Valerie's ex-girlfriend, which had been nightmarish. But once the play had started, the memory of Stacy was not enough of a cloud to darken her day.

Today is going to be just as great, she thought.

Amelia grabbed her phone to call Valerie, her mind on a coffee date, maybe a trip to the beach before getting ready for the show. But when she unlocked her phone, she saw an email from Valerie's boss, Matt, in her inbox already. It had been sent to her and her uncle at six in the morning.

Glen Packet, you have made such a tremendous impact on your community. We hope you are very proud of what you have been able to achieve. I see that the initial plan was to have a marketing agent onsite until the end of the performances; however, we are confident that the theatre will be able to flourish without an onsite employee. You will be refunded for the remainder of the onsite expenses and an itemized receipt is available upon request. I wish you all the best. Moving forward, please refer to your case manager Jorge for any of your future marketing needs.

Matt.

Amelia rolled her eyes. It wasn't her uncle who made the impact but it didn't really matter. She was more confused by the

change from Val to Jorge at the end of the process. There was also a text message from Valerie.

V: *I have to go. I'm so sorry, this wasn't how I wanted it to end. Break legs, Ames.*

Amelia felt gravity shift as her stomach sank. She tried to call Valerie, but the call went to voicemail.

"Hi there, you've reached Valerie Ross," her voice came through, "Sorry I missed your call. If this is urgent, please leave a message and I'll call you back as soon as possible. If you don leave a message, I'll assume it wasn't urgent. Thanks!"

There was a beep, and Amelia was at a loss for words. "Valerie?" She hung up and couldn't stop the tears welling up.

She called Jason. "I need you," she sobbed.

"I'm on my way," he said.

Amelia sunk to the floor and waited for her best friend to help her piece herself back together.

"This was not how I imagined the day," she said while picked out her clothes for the show. "Thank you for helping me."

"Of course. I wish I could heal the hurt you are feeling can make sure you look good." Jason picked out a cream-colored pant suit and a robin's egg blue bustier. "Y fierce and super fucking hot, and I mean that in the gayes possible," he put a hand up with his three middle fingers girl scout salute.

"I don't feel like it; fuck, it's so shitty."

"Yeah, what she did was shitty, but you are still a b with shit to do. So, we are going to go and get it done. (

Amelia nodded numbly.

"Okay," Jason continued, "we can wallow tomorro the show must go on."

Amelia rolled her eyes at the cliché.

Valerie knew she had won in the mother dep many of her peers had parents that did not accept the

religions, hobbies, careers... you name it. Her mother had been her number one fan in everything; when she wanted to play soccer, even though her mom knew nothing about sports, she was so proud. Or when Valerie decided to ditch the cleats for a clarinet- her mom was on board. She encouraged Valerie in every shifting fixation until Valerie discovered her true passion- photography. Granted, she currently used it for marketing and helping others with their businesses, and she loved what she did. But since she got trapped behind that desk, any dreams of opening her own photography business wilted and wilted until there was nothing left. This was all she focused on her whole drive back to Washington. If let herself think about Amelia, she'd call her. If she called, she'd turn around. Which meant that she'd probably get fired and lose her income.

So, when she got back into town, she went to her mom's house.

"I really hated leaving," she said over a bowl of mint and chip ice cream that they ate out of little blue glass dishes with little spoons. "I didn't tell her how I felt because I thought it would keep things simpler."

"Oh sweetheart," her mother replied. "Nothing is easy when it comes to feelings. Especially not ones with this much intensity. It's a romance that was stopped short, and that is hard to go through. I understand why you chose not to tell Amelia how you felt, but you do realize that your choice took hers away?"

Valerie shook her head, "Mom, it's not like she would want to have a long-distance relationship."

"Did you ask?"

"No."

"Well then how do you know?" Her mother helped herself to another scoop of ice cream. "You spent three weeks with this woman, and you think that's enough time for you to be able to make unilateral decisions on her life?"

"I did not..."

"Yes, you did. She told you how she felt about you, and you ran away."

"That's not what happened."

Elizabeth gave Valerie a knowing look, "Isn't it?"

"Well, technically yes, but not immediately like that."

"How else is she supposed to take it, Valerie?"

"I wanted to tell her, there wasn't a good time," Valerie pushed her ice cream around in her bowl. "You know how you talk about Dad? It's the closest to how I feel about her. But it's stupid, right? We live in different states. I have a stable job up here, and she has a career that she just poured her whole life into."

"And you cannot have a long-distance relationship because of what exactly?"

"Because… she's going to want someone else. We saw it happen with Stacy and she and I lived together!"

"So you rejected her before she could reject you."

"I did not reject her," Valerie said indignantly.

"You abandoned her," Elizabeth said with disapproval thick on her words.

"I had to come back! It wasn't my choice!"

"Enough!" Elizabeth said. "Valerie, my sweet child, you made the choice. Listen to me. You chose to leave and not say goodbye. You chose to run away from your own emotions. You chose that you'd rather let her take the fall than be vulnerable. You decided that. You are making the choice right now not to call her and explain."

Valerie checked the clock. "The show is still going on; she wouldn't be able to answer the phone anyway."

"But you could leave a message," Elizabeth said.

"I don't know what to say," Valerie said.

"Valerie, nothing you can do will ever stop me from loving you. But I am disappointed in you. I lost your father too early. I cannot get that time back. I hoped you would appreciate the time you have and use it to fill your life with love."

"That's not fair," Valerie protested.

"Life isn't fair. Don't let this pass you by; if you wait too long you'll miss it. Don't let this wrongdoing fester. The sooner you apologize and explain, the better it will be for your relationship."

Valerie got up to leave. "I have work tomorrow. Can I sleep here tonight? I don't know if Stacy is still at the apartment and honestly, I don't have it in me to deal with that right now."

Elizabeth sighed, "Of course you can stay here, wherever I live will always be your home. No matter how old you are."

"I love you, Mom. I'll think about what you said." With a hug and a kiss goodnight, Valerie went to her childhood bedroom. She lay in bed for a long while thinking about Amelia, about what she should say.

Her mother was right, inaction was a choice itself. Still, she could not bring herself to form the words.

Amelia was going through the motions. She was trying to hide how hard Valerie's absence was hitting her. It wasn't like Valerie had ever promised to stay. *Would she have stayed, if I had asked?*

Ticket sales had been strong. Nearly sold out every night, only ten to fifteen seats available. Uncle Glen was seemingly satisfied. Before the show had started, he had come up to her in the lobby. "I am very proud of you, Amelia. It looks like you have a good thing going here."

"Thanks," she said.

"We should have a celebratory dinner," he said. "Your brother will be arriving any moment. Ah, there he is."

"I was parking," Luke said, wrapping Amelia into a big hug. "Dude, this place is amazing! Look at this!"

"Dinner after the show sounds nice," Amelia said. Truthfully, she wanted to go home and go to sleep. Pretending not to be heartbroken was exhausting. She knew that going out to have a nice night with family would be better for her than going home and being lonely.

Uncle Glen wanted to have Mexican food, specifically Te Amo. They arrived and sat at a booth, but Amelia could see the table where she had been with Valerie and Elizabeth. Currently, two people were there on a date. Amelia knew they were on a date because they were playing footsies and had one hand holding the other person on top of the table.

"I just wanted to say again, I am so proud of you!" Luke said. "The theatre itself looks so good and the show was incredible too!"

"I admit I was skeptical, and I still have some concerns," Uncle Glen said, "but they come from a place of love. I just want to make sure you are going to be taken care of. After that horrendous scene at your opening night, I was convinced things would get worse for you. However, you handled it very well, and by intermission no one was talking about the wine in the programs incident. Honestly, if I had known that hiring a marketing professional was going to result in tabloid level dramatics, I would not have bothered. I called their office to report it. Do not worry, that Valerie character will not be handling any more cases and Jorge is the point of contact once again. I apologize for any distress Valerie caused, I feel responsible for allowing them to change agents last minute."

"Wait," Amelia said, "you called SPRUCE about Valerie's ex-girlfriend?"

"Oh, is that what it was about?"

"Her personal life is not her boss's business!"

"It is when it impacts her ability to do a job."

"Clearly it did not impact it very much though," Luke said, trying to mediate, "the sales seems great."

Amelia's mouth hung open in disbelief. "Did... did she get fired?" *If she got fired, should I call her?*

"I don't know. I think this was her first case, so they put her in a role that limited her contact with clients. I'm not surprised. She had green hair, Luke. What kind of professional dyes their hair?"

So, she's not fired, Amelia thought. *Should I call anyway? Just to check on her? To apologize for my uncle? No.*

She left without saying goodbye. Clearly, she doesn't want any contact with me.

"Lots of professionals have body mods. Dyed hair, tattoos, piercings… they have zero impact on someone's ability to work," Luke was saying.

"I am really glad you both came to see the show," Amelia wanted to change the subject. She did not want to think about Valerie's hair. "You guys should get season passes."

The men chuckled, "Nice sales pitch."

Chapter 29

The next morning Valerie woke up exhausted. Three weeks of working mostly in the evenings had caught up to her. It was six in the morning, and she was not ready to get out of bed. She smelt coffee coming from the kitchen. As she got ready for work, her mother left for her job at the middle school. "Have a good day, sweetheart."

When she arrived at the office, it was as if nothing around her had changed, and yet everything felt different. Had it always been so gloomy and grim in this building? The echo of the lobby with its sterile white walls was near haunting. Valerie walked through the cubical maze towards her desk. No one looked up or said hello to her. No one asked her how her trip was or how she was doing. *Maybe I wasn't crazy for feeling like an outsider. Does everyone in here feel this disconnected?*

Her office door was closed. She had to fish out her key from her bag because someone had locked it. As the lights turned on, Valerie could not believe what she saw. Her desk had become a dumping ground for three weeks' worth of backlogged edits. Her inbox on top of her desk was buried. She shuddered to imagine the inbox for her voicemail.

"Hey, Val, thanks for covering the theatre build for me." Jorge was standing in the door frame to her office with his hands in his pockets.

"Yeah, of course. I hope you are feeling better, Jorge."

"Oh, I am, thanks." He continued to stand in her doorway. "So, do you have the file?"

Valerie could feel the folio in her bag as if it were a part of her soul out of her body; like it was a lifeline to Amelia herself. There was no way in hell she was going to just hand it over to Jorge. It meant too much.

"Actually, I was going to talk to Matt about me keeping this one."

"Really?" Jorge's eyebrows rose. "That's not really your job though," he said in a condescending tone. "And besides," he took a bold step toward her and looked around her desk, "you seem to have a full plate." Maybe he noticed that he went a bit too far, or maybe he simply thought his point was made… but he turned to leave and said, "Drop it off by the end of the day, Val. I'd hate to see you drown in all that paperwork."

Valerie made her way over to Matt's office.

"Come in," Matt's voice dryly responded to her knock. "Ah, Valerie. Welcome back. How was everything with the build?"

"Everything went really well. I wanted- "

"Oh good. Jorge will have to maintain a very nice profile. Good job. We've missed you. So many little errors while you were gone."

"I want to keep the theatre account."

"Valerie. I think you are too attached, yes? See here."

Matt pulled up Instagram on his desktop. On the search for the theatre's location, there were a few hundred photos of the cast or taken by audience members. Matt clicked on one.

In this post, Valerie and Amelia were looking into each other's eyes in the skate rink. Valerie felt a pang in her chest. This was when Amelia was singing to her.

"See?" Matt said. "You're better off in editorial."

Valerie could not take one more day fixing everyone else's mistakes.

"Maybe if everyone else cared just a little bit more, I would not have to pick up their slack. If each marketing agent out there cared, there would not be a mountain on my desk that I guarantee is full of blatantly careless mistakes. Careless. And with all due respect, I was hired to be a marketing agent, to have my own clients; not to be grammar police for a bunch of asshats who couldn't care less!"

Matt did not seem to appreciate her dramatic yet passionate display (outburst). "You were hired to work here. You are assigned tasks and you complete them. You do your job well, and that is why you continue to do it. Maybe sending you on this build was a mistake. You have quite adequately displayed in your hysterics that you are not fit for a marketing position. End of discussion."

Matt turned his attention back to his computer. Valerie could not move. She was stunned. She did not want to give up, but what else could she do? She kept looking at Matt's wedding ring, and then she thought about Amelia. How Amelia juggled a million different hats and pulled off amazing things. How she too could do more if given the chance.

Later, Valerie would try and pinpoint exactly what triggered her decision.

"No," she said, "I have more to say. I want to be promoted to a marketing position. Yes, or no?"

Matt sputtered, not used to having his authority blatantly disregarded. "Valerie, you cannot just demand-"

"Matt, I've worked here for four years and if you have no intention of advancing me, then I am going to advance my career somewhere else."

"There are no open positions, maybe in a year or so..."

But Valerie was already done. "I signed an at-will employment form when I started, as such I don't have to give you a notice. Today is my last day." She saw Matt's mouth drop and she turned on her heel and did not bother to close the door behind her. She packed her office and did not respond when Jorge asked for the file, she left it on her office chair. The walk to the elevator was... interesting. She looked ahead and felt everyone's eyes on her.

Thankfully, Valerie had enough in savings to float her through a few weeks rent. She stopped by the apartment and was thankful to find that Stacy was not there. After calling her landlord to let him know that she would not be renewing her lease next month, she started packing her stuff, sorting what to sell, what to donate, and what to keep. A day went by before Valerie could work up the nerve to call Amelia, to try and explain or apologize. When the call picked up, Valerie was so relieved.

"I… honestly do not even know what to say. Ames, I…"

"You have got some nerve calling here." It was Jason.

"Jason, listen."

"No. I thought you were going to be good for her. You fucked up, just taking off like that on Friday."

"Jason."

"And you barely call her now? It's Tuesday! Fucking four days later," Jason's disappointment was like gravel.

"I'm moving down there. I want to make it right. I know I messed up, but I love her." Valerie said.

There was silence on the line.

"She's in the shower right now. You better explain good and fast."

So, she did. She explained how she was called back to work, how she didn't want to ruin Amelia's great mood with the sudden news that she was leaving. She explained how she was scared to call, ashamed. Valerie told Jason about how she quit her job, and how she was getting out of her lease on her apartment.

"I want to make things right with Ames," she finished.

"To be honest, I don't know how that is going to go. She hadn't opened up to anyone romantically in so long, and then she hands you her heart and you just leave it on the floor."

Valerie hated that he was right, she hated that she caused Amelia pain.

"I'm moving down there, it'll take me a week to get everything settled up here," Valerie said.

"The water stopped. I'll call you later," Jason said.

The call ended, and Valerie sat there with her phone in her hands. She called a florist in Oceanside to send a dozen red roses to Amelia's apartment.

Chapter 30

"She left, without saying goodbye. She left with just a fucking text!" Amelia exploded; she was getting more frustrated. "I mean, why wasn't she just honest with me?"

"Amelia," Jason said, "would you have given her a chance?"

Amelia sat down, deflated. The dozen red roses on the counter had just been delivered with a simple note.

Your favorite flowers
I'm sorry

From
V, not a disfigured French man

"I'm just saying, there was a lot going on for you that weekend. V probably didn't want to add to that." Jason looked at the card again. "What the hell does this card mean?"

"It's an inside joke and I don't feel like explaining right now. And so what that I had stuff going on? That means ghosting me is the answer? She should have just told me."

"Hey, I'm not saying the woman was smart about it." Jason raised his hands in surrender. "But have you talked to her at all since?"

Amelia pouted, in an obvious *no*. "Whatever, I thought she was… I thought we were at least friends."

"I am telling you this as your best friend, as the person who has known you longer than everyone else except your brother."

"My brother from another mother," Amelia added.

"You two looked at each other a little too long to just be friends. I know you aren't telling me everything, because if this was just friendship you would not be feeling this way."

Amelia adjusted her ponytail. "It doesn't matter. It's not like she's ever coming back."

"What if she did?" Jason asked. "What if she walked in and told you she wanted you."

She shrugged. "Life isn't a romance novel, Jason. Grow up." Jason gave her a look. "Okay, fine," she cradled her head in her hands. "If Valerie came back, I would want to give her a chance. But she would need to be honest with me. Long distance is hard enough. I need to feel secure; you know? I don't just want to be a flash in the pan to make her ex-girlfriend regret cheating. Not that I think that's what happened… I just… You know how my brain runs away with me, thinking of every possible reasoning and motive."

"I am very much aware that you are a Virgo, Amelia."

"My point is," Amelia tried to wrangle her thoughts into order, "I have to know that she's serious about me. I do not fool around with every pretty girl I meet. You know that's not me."

"It could be. You are hot enough and girls are always hitting on you," Jason said.

"I could in theory, but I couldn't in reality. I just don't feel comfortable with it. And I think that's the worst part of Valerie leaving like she did. It makes me feel like I am not worth more than a fling. I don't want to be flung around; I want a love that feels like a soft place to land. A love that goes down to the bones and becomes part of you."

"I know you do, Amelia."

Amelia took a deep breath and looked around the apartment. "I think I need to move." Jason looked at her puzzled. "I can't really afford this place on my own, and it's too big."

"How about we take this week and move all the theatre stuff out of your apartment and back to the theatre," Jason said. "How much longer do you have on your lease?"

"Three months."

Jason nodded. "Alright, so let's get your shit organized and sorted. You've got time."

"Alright."

"And maybe," he pushed the card back over to her, "you should call Valerie and let her know you got the flowers."

Amelia gave him a half smile. "Maybe you can mind your business."

Over the next week, Valerie had a single red rose delivered every day to Amelia's apartment. Each with a different card. Each of them an apology. Amelia did not call.

There was so much to do. Valerie had double checked, and triple checked that she had prepared all she could. The moving company had packed up all her belongings and she had a warranty for the storage unit.

"It is a big jump, sweetie," her mom had said, "Are you sure?"

"I see your concern and I know it's sudden and it's a huge change... but I already have three interviews set up for next week. And I love her, but I'm not moving for her, exactly. It's mostly for me. She might be the catalyst, but this is a good move for me. You know how miserable I was there; this is a new start. And now you can come visit me by the beach whenever you want!"

"I love you, my little pot of gold," her mom replied, "and I am excited for you. Worried, of course. But I am your mom, I will always worry about you. I'm glad that you're making amends. If California is good for you, then do what you need to do. I am proud of you; no matter what."

Along the drive, once again down the 5, Valerie thought about all the ways Amelia could respond to her showing back up. She might scream, which would be valid, she might give Valerie the cold shoulder... also valid. The outcome Valerie feared most was that Amelia was done. She hadn't responded to a single rose.

Either way, she had to see it through. The show must go on.

Chapter 31

Closing night of *Into the Woods* was sold out. Valerie was thankful to have a crowd to blend into. A few times, Amelia had almost spotted her. She hid like a coward.

I am not a coward, she thought to herself. Then she sat in the bathroom to avoid being seen.

A few minutes before showtime, Jason sent a text.

J: *Are you here?*

She sent back a quick reply.

V: *Yes.*
V: *I am hiding in the bathroom. I need help, I brought her flowers and I do not want her to notice them.*

A few moments passed. Valerie wished she had grabbed a drink to calm her nerves but thought about all the germs in the bathroom.

A new text from Jason.

J: *Okay, I have her in the green room to give the cast a closing night pep talk. I will come meet you in the lobby and grab them.*

Valerie left the bathroom stall she was hiding in. Even though she hadn't used the bathroom, she washed her hands. Thinking about all the germs had really gotten to her. She ran outside to her car and grabbed the bouquet of a dozen red roses. Jason was waiting for her in the lobby.

"One more thing!" She grabbed the little comedy and tragedy masks enamel pin and attached it to the periwinkle ribbon wrapped around the stems of the roses before handing them over fully. "Okay, should I sit now or wait?"

Jason thought for a moment, "I think the house is full enough that she won't see you. Just keep your nose in the program and it should be fine. The wig is a nice touch," he teased.

Valerie followed him into the audience. He climbed the steps up to the booth. Her seat was in the fifth row. Hopefully she could keep the surprise.

The lights dimmed over the seats and the audience hushed in preparation. A single spotlight center stage was ready for when Amelia stepped into it. Valerie's heart felt as though it had been struck like a gong. How was it possible for Amelia to have gotten more beautiful in the last week?

"Thank you all for attending closing night of *Into the Woods*," Amelia said. "This has been a really big passion project for all of us involved. From the cast and crew and production teams, we hope you all enjoy it. If you haven't had a chance, during intermission or after the show we have a raffle for some season passes. This is the start of a wonderful season," the audience cheered. Valerie could see the mist in Amelia's eyes. She was surprised to be tearing up too. She had done it! Amelia had successfully launched her dream, and in doing so, brought people together to create art. It was beautiful and inspiring. Valerie could hardly wait to tell her that she had been inspired too; to finally take the leap of faith into her own creative career.

But she had to wait still; to wait two acts and an intermission. She wanted to think about all the ways their interaction could go. To think and prepare and plan for each reaction. Would she be happy? Angry? Confused? Forgiving?

But as soon as the curtain opened, Valerie decided instead to let herself be swept away. She took a deep breath in, and then let it out. There was nothing she could do until after curtain call, and even then, all she could do was apologize and be open. So, she let herself be pulled into the woods.

At intermission, Valerie rushed out to the bathrooms. By now, Amelia had seen the flowers and might be looking for her.

She texted Jason a toilet emoji.

He sent back a laughing crying face, followed by a "She's in the back room, you can go back to your seat."

Valerie decided to take a gamble and buy a glass of champagne first.

After the show, Valerie was the last audience member to leave for the lobby. Amelia was there, in her beautiful lilac dress and green olive Doc Martens. Her face mask had embroidered clouds. She was wearing purple mascara and the small enamel pin of the masks was just beneath her left collarbone.

"Great show," Valerie said.

"You *are* here!" Amelia exclaimed, almost accusatory. She grabbed "I thought, maybe Jason had put the flowers there or someone from the cast." Then a cloud covered the sun in her eyes, and she took a step back. "Are you here for work?"

Valerie grabbed her hand, "No." Amelia waited, so she continued. "I am here because… I quit." Clouds turned to lightning, brilliant and scary.

"You *what*?"

"I quit the company. They… I didn't… You inspired me."

"I don't understand." Amelia said. "I told you I loved you and you just… disappeared. You didn't even say goodbye."

"I know, and I will never be able to say sorry enough. It was horrible, *I* was horrible. But," Amelia pulled her in for a hug. "Ames, I never wanted to hurt you. I got called back to work and I did not know how to tell you I was leaving, especially when I did not want to go."

187

"Wait, you quit your job?" Amelia pulled back. She looked worried. "That's a lot; if you did all that for *me*, I mean, I'd be flattered but that's kind of... intense." She half laughed.

"And I started looking for apartments," Valerie said. "I got an Airbnb for now, and I have a few job interviews lined up... Amelia..." She puts up a hand to stop her from interrupting, "Please let me finish. I know it's a lot but I did not move here for you."

Amelia raised a skeptical eyebrow.

"You were a catalyst, not the cause. Does that make sense? My dream is to be a photographer. To capture moments and frame them. Since I've been down here, my photography business has thrived. I mean, it really took off. You inspired me to chase my dream with the same tenacity that you achieved yours."

"So, not for me?" Amelia teased. "You sure know how to make a girl feel special."

Valerie laughed. "Not for you, although being closer to you is a wonderful benefit. And I will do anything legal to prove how I feel to you."

"And how do you feel, V?" The space between them was shrinking, they were both moving closer together. Valerie's hand was on Amelia's cheek, leaning in.

"You know," she said.

"What changed?"

"I got to thinking, and I did not want to get old and think of you as the right person at the wrong time. So, I decided to make this the right time," Valerie said.

Then they closed the distance and kissed.

They were both shaking from the anticipation. The moment their lips touched was like a tidal wave. It drowned out everything around them. To both, it felt like home.

Final Bows

Amelia never thought she'd need a partner in life, but with Valerie, it was not just a need. It was about want. She wanted to spend every single day with this wonderful woman. This woman who believed in her, who inspired her, who knew her. In one short year, they had become closer than anyone else. When she had a hard day at the theatre, Valerie would be there to listen to her. She would offer help when needed, but always an unwavering amount of support. They had found a routine. Amelia with the theatre, Valerie with her photography business. Her apartment had gone from a lonely resting place to a home of two female entrepreneurs. It housed love. No matter how busy they got, they made sure to spend time together. Even if it was just folding the laundry together before bed, Amelia had come to treasure those moments.

Valerie was feeling the same way. She appreciated every little thing Amelia did for them. She always made sure that Valerie's camera batteries were charging at the end of the day. Valerie had been able to book photography sessions in the early evenings at golden hour while Amelia started rehearsals. Then after a session, Valerie would swing by the theatre to drop off some dinner. Sometimes she would stay and edit photos in the office of the theatre, sometimes she would go home.

Faster than it seemed possible, it was time to announce the official second season of The Rose Theatre.

The theatre was decorated with creamy tulle and fairy lights. Amelia and Valerie wanted an airy, sparkling champagne theme. Cast and crew members from each show of the season had been invited, along with season pass holders and a few other guests. Valerie was excited to have her mom in attendance in celebration.

"I'm so proud of you girls," Elizabeth said, giving them both a hug at once, kissing them each on the cheek.

"Our babies, you've done so well," Kennedy agreed. Rhett was sitting at the table, smiling and letting the women have their moment.

"Thanks, Aunt Kennedy, and thanks Liz," Amelia said.

They turned to make rounds and welcome people to the event, but Valerie looked back at Kennedy and Elizabeth and let them see the brimming excitement in her face. They gave her thumbs up in response and sat down at their table.

Luke strolled in with a woman on his arm that Amelia didn't recognize.

"Hey sis," Luke said, wrapping her into a bear hug, lifting her up. "Congrats on finishing the first year."

"Thanks," Amelia said.

"And you too, V! Hey, this is Georgie," he gestured to the woman next to him, "she's a model. For your photography stuff. Always networking." Georgie smiled and she and Valerie started talking. Amelia was pulled into another conversation with some of the actors who had become regulars at The Rose.

When she and Valerie were able to reconvene at the little stage, everyone was in attendance, and it was almost time to start the show.

"Relax, V. This is your night to enjoy yourself too." Amelia reminded her for the hundredth time.

Valerie kissed her on the forehead, "This night is a testament to all the work you've done. I am so fucking proud of you."

"I couldn't have done it without you," Amelia replied, giving Valerie's hand a squeeze.

"Yeah, you could've, but I'm grateful to have a part in it."

Jason and Austin were behind a DJ booth. Jason in a white suit, Austin in black. They were definitely the kind of couple to match at every event. Amelia was skeptical at first, but Austin had proven that he really cared for Jason. He had some internalized homophobia to work through and thanks to therapy and trust, Austin was able to come out as queer, incidentally during a production of *If/Then* where he played Lucas. The whole cast threw him a coming out party when he and Jason made their relationship public. Since then, Amelia has been absolutely overjoyed that Jason is happy. Jason and Austin recently moved in together and just adopted a grey kitten named Idina.

Valerie played a slideshow with some videos of the entire season, including some behind the scenes and rehearsal clips. There had been so much great footage to choose from. She sat there with her hand entwined with Amelia's. Valerie was watching her every reaction. At the end of it, Amelia's eyes were misty.

"Thank you, love." They walked up to the front of the party. Amelia read off the superlatives, which had been voted on as guests entered. As each winner was announced, Valerie handed them a star shaped enamel pin with the year engraved on it.

"Violet Honor, this award like the purple heart, goes to the actor who got hurt during a performance and kept the show rolling… to Isabella! Who accidentally broke a finger during Les Mis!" Everyone clapped, the award winner came forward, and on it went.

Amelia and Valerie, Jason and Austin had spent days trying to come up with as many awards as possible. Some were very specific, some were broader. But it was all for fun.

"Time to announce next year's season!" Amelia said. Valerie was nervous. So very nervous. "Valerie, if you'll play the video?" Valerie had been tasked with creating a video to present the new shows for the second ever season of The Rose Theatre." Jason and Austin nodded in encouragement to Valerie as she pressed play.

Each slide presented the title and poster art for a different show in the next season, along with the performance dates. The crowd cheered, everyone was excited for the different shows, and Valerie could tell Amelia was relieved that she had picked well.

Valerie stood side by side with Amelia as they watched the announcement video. At the end of the reveals, there was a firework graphic. Everyone clapped, including Amelia, who believed this was the end of the video. But then the music transitioned to a soft guitar melody.

"It was only in the theatre I truly lived!" appeared on screen. Jason had handed Valerie a microphone while Amelia was distracted by the surprise extended announcement video.

"A beautiful woman quoted Wilde on the second day I knew her," she said. Amelia looked at her, eyes wide, an uncomfortable smile on her face from so many people looking at her, it clearly said, "V, what are you doing?"

Valerie did not look at the crowd. She knew most of the people out there, but they weren't important right now.

"I did not know what she meant at the time. But this last year, Amelia has shown me what it means to find a family in a theatre, to find a home, to find myself. She also told me that she only liked surprises that are positive. It's no surprise that she has shown me what it means to love, to be loved. And I love her for it. I love you, Amelia."

The crowd collectively "awed" in response.

"You are the most driven, incredible woman I've ever known. You can take an idea and turn it into this," Valerie gestured toward the crowd, but did not dare look at them. Her eyes remained fixed on Amelia, and she did not want to risk a stage fright episode. "This community has blossomed because you gave it a space to. I have been changed because of you. You have made such a marvelous impact on everyone you interact with. And on top of your creativity, generosity, and compassion, you are my best friend. You're the one I turn to first when I have news, good or bad. You're the one I would want by my side in the darkest days. You're the one I want to dance with in the moments that feel like pure starlight. I love your smile, your laugh, how you follow your heart and trust your gut. You have taught me how to stick to my guns, and I am taking a page out of your book here- but my heart knows you. I will follow you through each scene and stage of our lives. They say, 'when you know, you know' and Amelia, darling Amelia, I have known in my soul since the beginning."

Valerie knelt on one knee, her palms were sweating, and Amelia's eyes were misty, but her smile. That beautiful fucking smile was worth the whole world. Gasps from the crowd. Valerie could hear the distinct sound of her mother practically cooing.

A small huff of laughter escaped Valerie's mouth right before she asked, "Amelia, will you marry me?"

The moment stopped. The music slowed. Valerie was only vaguely aware of the flashes of photography as Amelia nodded and let out a laugh of pure bubbling joy.

They kissed, and time sped up and crashed back in place all at once. Valerie slid the ring on Amelia's finger, a teardrop-shaped sapphire with small diamonds on either side.

"I love you, V."

"With my whole soul, Ames."

"She said yes!" Jason and Austin screamed as they turned on the bubble machines.

Laughter and tears of joy filled the air. Happily Ever After might not be as easy as people think, but with the right person at her side, Valerie knew that everything else would be okay. Life would get hard, messy, and scary. But they had each other to hold in those moments of doubt and darkness, and that would make all the difference.

Curtain.

Author Note

I started writing this book, not as a queer story, but a love story. There is a cast of queer characters, but so is life. I was very intentional about avoiding any kind of coming out story as a plot point. Coming out can be very traumatic and it is something that queer people must do over and over and over again. It never ends. Maybe someday it won't be necessary.

I call this book a sapphic romcom because while Amelia identifies as a lesbian, Valerie does not. She is content with the label "queer" and "gay" as umbrella terms that she fits within. Remember that not everyone wants or needs to label themselves. For some it's natural to do so, but not for everyone. Don't push people into boxes they don't want to be in.

One thing I wanted to note on was the subplot of Jason and Austin. I did have sensitive readers for the transgender issues in this book. One of the comments I got from cis-gendered beta readers was "I was surprised that Jason was trans! I didn't see that coming!" That was intentional. Jason is Amelia's friend. He works as a techie for The Rose Theatre. There's history between him and Austin. These are the important facts of Jason for our main character Valerie. Jason is passing, and he's happy to be mistaken as a cis-man. There are many people who are very vocal about being trans, and that's amazing! But there are also a large group of trans people who don't. I did not want Jason to be a token trans character, he's a character who just so happens to be transgender.

If you are questioning your gender identity or sexuality, then I wish you luck on your journey! Everyone's path is unique. Make sure you have someone safe to talk to.

Theatre opens up a whole world of community and family to Valerie, as it has done for me and so many others. Take a moment to see a show at the local community theatres in your area! Ames and V would be glad you did.

Acknowledges

Writing is often a solitary task, but publishing a book is not. There are so many people who went on this journey with me.

First, I want to thank Jacob. You, who listened to me complain and gripe when I was frustrated or overwhelmed. You, who made sure I always had food. You, who gave me space to create. You, who told me over and over that you believe in me. This book exists because you gave me the safety and space to create it.

Next, my human sound boards and feedback readers: Ty, Karen, James, Krista, Sylvia, Kylie, and Krisi. For listening to me every time I call or text and have a new idea, and all the venting and ranting I do. You guys are amazing for taking the time to read through rough versions of this story with patience.

The team over at Birdcage Ink for taking a chance on me and this book.

Madi at Love Lee Creative for my cover!

Thank you also to my friends on bookstagram! I created my account @stephaniejeanbooks when I was going through the depths of postpartum and found community there. You guys are so freaking cool and I am very happy to be part of it.

Another shoutout to the ladies I met at Charm City RomantiCon in Maryland March 2023. You guys were the first people to hear the title of this book (especially Sandy and Charmaine, who hyped me up as I decided it over drinks). Your enthusiasm fueled me. I'm so grateful to have met you!

To the readers. Thank you so much for reading this book. It's like when the Rose Theatre has the first audience on opening night. Without an audience, it's just rehearsal. Books are written for the readers. So, this is for you. See you in the next one!

And finally, once again to Jacob and Hazel. Because you two are the reason behind everything I do. I love you.

More from Stephanie Jean

HI, I'M STEPHANIE!
I'M A CALIFORNIA GIRL WHERE I LIVE WITH
MY PARTNER AND OUR LITTLE GOBLIN.
PISCES SUN, PISCES MOON, AND LIBRA
RISING – IF YOU CARE TO KNOW.
I'M A SWIFTIE AND MY COMFORT SHOWS ARE
GILMORE GIRLS AND AVATAR: THE LAST
AIRBENDER.
I LOVE THEATRE AND BOOKS (OBVIOUSLY)
AND THE PINK DRINK SHADE OF PINK IS MY
FAVORITE COLOR.
FOLLOW ME ON BOOKSTAGRAM WHERE I
POST MOST CONSISTENTLY OR MY
FACEBOOK READER GROUP "STEPHANIE JEAN
READER GROUP"

@STEPHANIEJEANBOOKS

BIRDCAGEINK.COM